LIFE A
POLITICAL
REALITY

It's good to read works outside the sphere of the Anglophone and the European, not because we perform a duty by doing so, but because, as with these arresting novellas by Shahidul Zahir, they amplify our sense of what fiction can do. Zahir's world is close, sometimes violent, but never claustrophobic. It enables discovery, even love, showing us the curiously moving ways in which human beings assign value to small things, including their own lives. – AMIT CHAUDHURI

In these novellas the political is the personal is the intimate is the lyrical is the ironic is the universal. Perhaps it would be best if you were to read these books which will leave you with unforgettable images of a jamdani of skulls and a flock of sarus cranes as harbingers of a nation in the throes of birth. – JERRY PINTO

Zahir's writing is propelled by an alertness to the inner lives of objects, animals, the landscape, and marginalized people as they collide against the obscene lies created by those in power. Haunting and apocalyptic, his fiction may be about the recent past, but it reads like a literature of the future. – SIDDHARTHA DEB

SHAHIDUL ZAHIR

LIFE AND POLITICAL REALITY: TWO NOVELLAS

TRANSLATED FROM
THE BENGALI BY
V. RAMASWAMY & SHAHROZA NAHRIN

HARPER**PERENNIAL**

An Imprint of HarperCollins Publishers

First published in English in India by Harper Perennial 2022
An imprint of HarperCollins *Publishers*
4th Floor, Tower A, Building No. 10, Phase II, DLF Cyber City,
Gurugram – 122002
www.harpercollins.co.in

2 4 6 8 10 9 7 5 3 1

Originally published in Bengali as
Jibon O Rajnoitik Bastobota © Shahidul Zahir 1987
Abu Ibrahimer Mrityu © Shahidul Zahir 1991
This English translation © V. Ramaswamy and Shahroza Nahrin 2022
Translator's Afterword © V. Ramaswamy 2022

P-ISBN: 978-93-5489-230-1
E-ISBN: 978-93-5489-237-0

Cover design: Twisha Mehta

Typeset in 11.5/16.2 Adobe Caslon Pro at
Manipal Technologies Limited, Manipal

Printed and bound at
Thomson Press (India) Ltd

 HarperCollinsIn

For Iqbal Hasnu

Contents

Life and Political Reality

ONE DAY IN 1985, THE sandal on the foot of Abdul Mojid, a young man from Lakshmi Bazar's Shyama Prosad Chowdhury Lane, lost conformity with circumstances and went *phot* and snapped. Actually, if the theory of the life of matter had been scientifically established, perhaps it could have been said that the strap of the sponge sandal on his right foot snapped not because of the failure of matter, but rather, on account of that inner reason for which, soon after this, his very being sought to fall apart all over again. The strap of his sandal snapped while he was on the way to Raysha Bazar; he had just reached Nawabpur Road after emerging from Karkunbari Lane, and so he stopped and stood there. That was when, within the noise and chaos of the crowds and vehicles of Nawabpur Road, he perceived something more. Going beyond the sounds that men and vehicles make, to which men are not always alert, he entered the sphere of a tinnitus. He observed that the lacklustre afternoon sky above Nawabpur was clouded by termites, and that there were countless crows gambolling behind the fleeing termites. It occurred to him that because of the screeches of the crows and the soundless striving of the termites to escape, a kind of silent panic pervaded the melancholy afternoon at Nawabpur Road. His senses then became alert to something else; he heard the sound of a loudspeaker close by. Like every other person present at that moment on Nawabpur Road, he looked towards the source of the sound, and there, in front of him, across the road, next to the Police Club, he spotted Abul Khayer with a microphone in his hand. Abdul Mojid saw Abul Khayer sitting on a stationary rickshaw and speaking with a microphone held near his mouth, his words emanating explosively from the large speaker placed atop the hood of the rickshaw. Training his sight on the crows and termites, Abdul Mojid then listened, for those few moments, to what Abul Khayer was saying. Everyone walking along Nawabpur Road at the time understood what he was saying. Abul Khayer said, 'Aapneder dhonnyobad. I thank you all.' Everyone figured out what he meant by this, without much thought or analysis. Because all those who heard him knew exactly what he was referring to. They knew that, amidst the screeching of crows and the noise of vehicles, Abul Khayer was now thanking everyone for the strike called by various parties that had taken place the previous day. It occurred to Abdul Mojid that his heart had been riven for a long time, but that day, in the melancholy afternoon of the carnival of termite slaughter, hearing what Abul Khayer uttered, his heartstrings, like the strap of his sandal, snapped once again. When Abdul Mojid cast his eyes on Abul Khayer's long and youthful beard and on his blue-coloured jobba, he imagined that it was from inside

Abul Khayer's jobba that all the crows had emerged. He thought these were *those* crows; after all, he knew about Abul Khayer's intimacy, through family association, with crows. What a mysterious, secret love for crows his father, Moulana Bodruddin, had. The people of Lakshmi Bazar remembered that in 1971, come evening, Moulana Bodu used to smile tenderly and set crows flying in the moholla's sky. Moulana Bodu and his sons used to go up to his rooftop with a plateful of meat. Those who were still there in the moholla then had said that the meat, whose pieces Moulana Bodu flung skywards every day, was human flesh. Because the head of the oldest Muslim family of the moholla, Khwaja Ahmed Ali, had said that one day when the crows failed to grab a piece of meat that had been thrown, it landed on the roof of his house. Sitting on his rooftop under a shaft of late afternoon sunlight, he was immersed in the remembrance of his bygone youth when the piece of meat fell near his feet. He observed it for a while and realized that the skin was intact on one side of the piece of flesh, and he saw that this skin was extremely smooth. Everyone in the moholla learnt about all this later. That same evening, holding the piece of flesh in his hand, he saw that there was a floral gemstone on it, the size of a grain of dal. He wailed out, and holding the piece in the cup of his hands, he descended the stairs, and with the help of his elder son, Khwaja Shofiq, buried it in the courtyard of his own house with due obsequies. After that, while offering the Maghrib prayers, he sobbed inconsolably. The heart of a sad old man from Lakshmi Bazar broke that day on account of an unknown girl. Now, the twin graves of Khwaja Ahmed Ali and his son lay in the courtyard of his house. Another piece of flesh, from the big toe of a foot, had been found by an unknown pedestrian on the pavement beside the road. Abu Korim's elder son had witnessed it, and so people came to know all about it. The nail of the toe was long and hard, and there was a thick tuft of hair over it. A bright red nail polish had been applied on it. Hearing about the nail polish, everyone thought it to be a woman's toe, but after hearing about the tuft of hair, everyone concluded it belonged to a man. Subsequently, everyone presumed it to be a hijra's. No one knew what happened to this severed toe. But one day, Abu Korim's elder son disappeared while returning from a shop in Raysha Bazar. Another piece of flesh had fallen beside the well of Jomir Byapari's house, right into the rice pot, while rice was being washed in the late afternoon. It was a severed penis. When it fell into the pot, Jomir Byapari's teenage daughter was startled, but when she fished the thing out from the pot, she couldn't recognize what it was. When she took it to her Ma, Byapari's wife recognized the object on account of experience. The severed penis was circumcised, shorn. Seeing that, Byapari's wife was dumbfounded. Even though her daughter was going, 'What's this, Ma? What's this, Ma?' she didn't tell her anything. She wrapped the severed male member in a rag and kept it aside. When the rag was unwrapped and the thing was shown to Jomir Byapari after he returned home at night, he became enraged with his wife as well as everyone else. Then, when his daughter asked in whispers what the thing was, he blurted out, '*Lyaoda!* A bloody dick!' But the girl still could not recognize the thing and she thought her father had sworn at her because he was in a foul mood. After that, Jomir Byapari went to Moulana Bodu's house that very night and delivered the member wrapped in the rag. The people of the moholla learnt in detail about all this. As soon as Moulana Bodu's second and young wife, Lotifa, who was sitting in front of him, unwrapped the gift and revealed it, she threw it away, saying, 'Ae Ma, it looks like a leech!' But Moulana Bodu did not rise from the cot even after that. Young Lotifa then switched on the light, poked it using the sharp end of a pencil and recognized the thing, and that was when Moulana Bodu asked her what it was. When his wife failed to respond and remained silent, he rose and bent down and saw the terrifying organ. His wife then spoke, 'It's a Muslim's.' Hearing that, Moulana Bodu remained silent. It was not initially clear why Moulana Bodu fell silent, but he was definitely not perturbed because the body part belonged to a Muslim. In fact, in 1971, after the Liberation War began, the first person to be killed in the moholla had been a Muslim and a minor. Moulana Bodu had no reason to remember that fact, but the people of the moholla remembered it. All their lives, they remembered that the first person who had been killed in the moholla in 1971 was Alauddin, who used to work in the motor garage, and according to his Ma's calculations, had turned thirteen on the day he was killed. After Alauddin died, the people of the moholla also remembered – and they still do – that Moulana Bodu had flown into a rage one day when his eyes fell upon Alauddin's penis while he was pissing against the wall with one leg of his pair of shorts rolled up: '*Haramjada, kharaya kharaya motoch, kharaya mote kutta.* Bastard, you're pissing standing up, it's dogs that stand and piss.' What Alauddin then did sealed his fate, and he was killed cruelly a few days later. When he heard what Moulana Bodu said, he first mocked him by rolling his tongue around inside his cheek, then said, '*Kutta to mukh diya khaibi, apne awkonthon hoga diya khayen.* But dogs also eat with their mouths, you should start eating through your arse from now on.' When his father heard him say this obscene thing to Moulana Bodu, he tied him to a guava tree and gave him a sound hiding, and as Alauddin kept screaming, '*Aar korum na, aar korum na.* I won't do it again, I won't do it again,' the people of the moholla came to know all about it. Three months and nine days after this, one afternoon, when the people of the moholla were running like termites chased by crows, screaming, '*Militari aise, militari aise!* The army's here, the army's here!' – the day Moulana Bodu and Captain Imran first discovered one another – Alauddin's lifeless body was found in the moholla, face upwards, after it landed up on the lane in front of his house. And therefore, it could be said that when Moulana Bodu saw the severed penis and fell silent, it was not because he heard his wife say that the organ belonged to a Muslim. Very late that night, after a long spell of coming to terms with himself and after he had shed all his cowardice, he arrived at a response relating to the fundamental aspect of his discomfiture regarding what Lotifa had said. He realized that Lotifa had not just beheld a man's sexual organ, she had also displayed a lot of eagerness in that regard; she had identified it as a man's sexual organ. And she hadn't just stopped there, she had identified it as belonging to a Muslim. Once Moulana Bodu had resolved the matter, his gloomy silence vanished. He woke Lotifa up and divorced her right there by uttering 'talaq' thrice. Although many people had fled the moholla by then, those who remained found out about everything in detail subsequently. The truth behind everything came to be established. Because the next day, Moulana Bodu's second and young wife left the house, but before that, all night long, the sad and relentless sound of a woman weeping kept everybody in Lakshmi Bazar awake. Not a single person stepped out of their house. Even as they lay in bed without turning their lights on, the moholla's remaining folk identified that it was Moulana Bodu's second wife, the beautiful, rustic young Lotifa who was weeping; she was in some kind of distress. Everyone stayed

awake in the darkness, but at one point, when the boy
Abdul Mojid could bear it no more, he switched on the
light momentarily. The next morning, when Abdul Mojid's
Ma went to Moulana Bodu's house, he told all the people
gathered there that nothing had happened. He praised God
and thanked everybody. But he conducted himself
differently with two people from among those who came.
First, he told Abdul Mojid's widowed Ma that, of all the
people in this moholla, it was only they who still had the
nerve. Second, he suddenly landed a slap on Jomir Byapari's
woebegone face, but he didn't say a single word to him. The
people present there looked on in dazed astonishment, the
way entranced spectators gaze at a magician's inexplicable
act and try to figure it out. But they couldn't comprehend,
they merely watched in silence. Although Jomir Byapari
had been slapped and Abdul Mojid's Ma praised,
nonetheless, the people saw the same kind of gloom writ
large on both their faces, and they sensed the same kind of
fear in the minds of both people. Jomir Byapari had been
able to glimpse what was inside Moulana Bodu through
the chance opportunity of the momentary collapse of all his
solemnity and sense of determination, something he had
rapidly attained after overcoming the extreme anxiety and
sense of inferiority that he had felt in the days preceding
the 25th of March. But before another morning could
dawn, Jomir Byapari slung a padlock on the door of his
house and disappeared for seven and a half months with his

wife and children. He got away with a slap, but Abdul Mojid's Ma was unable to protect her family from calamity. Terrified by Moulana Bodu's praise, the widowed lady returned home and related to her children the very thing that Moulana Bodu had told her: '*Koilo, mohollar bhitre apnegoi awkhono sahos aase, kyan koilo?* He said, it's only you people in this moholla who still have the nerve, why did he say that?' None of her four children could tell her why he had said that. They merely kept it in mind and felt imperilled, like their Ma. They couldn't find any element of audacity in their household; the elderly man of the family had been dead for five years now, the only son of the household was merely fourteen years old, and the eldest daughter was twenty and still unmarried. Such a family was thrown into chaos on account of the accusation of audacity. The brow of the boy Abdul Mojid was furrowed all day, and after that, come dusk, he looked at his Ma and elder sister and said, 'Forget about it, I tell you, forget about it.' He said it in a way that suggested he had assumed his Ma and sister were as worried about the matter as he was, and he realized that his assumption was correct. Because, hearing him, his sister replied, '*Haw, ei loya bhabichh na.* Yes, don't worry about this.' But Abdul Mojid felt that there was no end to the anxiety. After that, at various stages in his life he realized that the thing, which on that terrifying day in his boyhood he had said should be forgotten, had in fact not been forgotten in any way, and that's why, fifteen years later, hearing the words of Moulana Bodu's son, Moulana Khayer, who was wearing the same kind of jobba, Abdul Mojid gave up the shopping trip to Raysha Bazar, returned home with the torn sandal in his hand, and gazed at his wife Yasmin's face. He saw that a vein at the base of Yasmin's bony shoulder was throbbing; he touched the spot with his finger. A bayonet had been pierced in such a spot near Momena's neck. Casting his eyes on his wife's face, he once again remembered the subject of audacity and cowardliness. Abdul Mojid knew, and for that matter, even before attaining puberty he had realized the secret, that he, his Ma and his sister despised Moulana Bodu. And perhaps that was what Moulana Bodu had indicated to his Ma on the morning of the day his wife left the house. Abdul Mojid realized that even after stepping into adulthood, he was a weak sort of man, he was fearful and always somewhat anxious; but despite all that, he could not forget about the hate, and when he gazed at Yasmin's face, his hatred turned to rage. Perhaps Moulana Bodu had glimpsed this rage which burned like cold fire, perhaps he still did. Abdul Mojid realized that this audacious hatred had somehow turned his timid life topsy-turvy. He wanted to surrender himself to Yasmin's embrace and find tranquillity. He thought to himself, '*Ei dyasher mainshere ayalay Bodu Moulanar polay koy, bhaichhab*. So Moulana Bodu's son now addresses the people of this country as "brothers". *Koy, apnego dhonnyobad*. He says, "I thank you all."' Like a fevered soul, Abdul Mojid sobbed out, 'Aapa, Aapa,' throwing his arms around Yasmin. He felt ashamed of his timidity, but he couldn't do anything. He realized it was necessary to be brave. But he could not find the means to be brave; all his life he kept feeling the need to muster up courage. The day the boy Abdul Mojid had first felt the need to be brave, he decided that he would become a goonda. When he was studying in class eight in the Collegiate School, the day Moulana Bodu swore at Momena on the street, he thought that the only way he could avenge it was by becoming a goonda; at the time, Momena was the only Muslim girl in this locality of Lakshmi Bazar who used to sing. She was friends with Basanti Gomez. And Basanti Gomez used to take her along to the church in St Gregory's School to join the choir. When Momena was returning after singing at an event at Silverdale School in Wari, Moulana Bodu swore at her as he went past. That day, after returning home, Momena had trembled in the throes of an extraordinary agony and had sobbed and wailed, *'Koy ki, dim parbar jao. Haramir pola amare koy ki, magi, dim parbar jao.* He said, "Do you go to lay eggs?" The son of a bastard tells me, "You whore, do you go to lay eggs?"' Seeing his Momena Aapa in such a state, it had seemed to Abdul Mojid that she was like a chicken that had been butchered and laid under an upturned basket by the side of the well. Standing outside the door, Abdul Mojid had then become aware of the feeling whose name was hate, and he was assailed by an emotion – that of revenge. The boy Abdul Mojid had felt that he wanted to take revenge for the insult to his Momena Aapa, *'Kandich na aapa, mandarpor thota phataya diya amune!* Don't cry, Aapa, I'll smash that swine's face!' But he hadn't exactly figured out how he would do that, and at that very moment, he also discovered the feeling that was called cowardice. Confronting this feeling, Abdul Mojid decided that he would become a goonda like Korim, and that he would stand with his legs splayed out and play the guitar like Basanti Gomez's brother, Pankaj Gomez. But in the end, he couldn't do anything at all. For a few days, he tried to find out the way to become a goonda: he puffed cigarettes with Korim, and seeing girls, he puckered his lips and whistled. But he was soon bored with all that, and he was also unable to move ahead on account of his Ma and Momena. Finding cigarettes in his pocket, his Ma admonished him, and after that Momena sat beside his cot, and stroking his head, reminded him of his responsibilities, *'Tui emun koroch! Tor upre mar koto asha, tui poirashuina koto boro hobi.* You do such things! Ma has such high hopes for you, that you'll get educated and become a big man.' Abdul Mojid gazed at Momena's face and remained silent, and then he remembered Momena's anguish – *'Koy ki, dim parbar jao, magi.* He says, "Do you go to lay eggs, you whore?"' The boy Abdul Mojid's eyes were full of tears that day. It seemed he was observing the verdant earth from beneath salty water; he beheld his Momena Aapa's face. From the depths of the anguish he felt in his heart, he sensed love for the first time in his life. Burying his face in the folds of Momena's sari, he hugged her – a Momena whom he did not yet know, whom he would discover dead, with a gaping wound from a bayonet that had pierced the left side of her neck, near her shoulder, and her face lying aslant. The look in his Ma's eyes and the scent of the starch on Momena Aapa's sari didn't allow Abdul Mojid to become a goonda, and any remaining possibility of that came to naught when, following good results in the annual examination at school, he was promoted to class nine, and Basanti Gomez opened the doors of her family library to him. He discovered dust and the smell of naphthalene inside Basanti Gomez's books, and after a time it occurred to him that there was no way he could stand at the crossroads at the end of the street and swear at Moulana Bodu, calling out, *'Mandarpo!* You swine!' Moulana Bodu became Abdul Mojid's enemy the day he had said foul things to his sister and she had moaned in the throes of unbearable anguish, and he became the entire moholla's enemy in 1971, in the days after the sky came alight with the blazing flames of Nayabazar. He suddenly arrived then with a black-checked scarf thrown over his shoulders, and seeing him beside the Punjabi soldiers, the people of the moholla couldn't figure out whether or not he was Bengali, and those people of Lakshmi Bazar who remained until the

end saw him flying his crows the whole year. They saw how
the quivering creases on Moulana Bodu's face in the
beginning of 1971 became tranquil after the 25th of March,
and how he was discovered by the army the day they first
arrived in the moholla. That day, after a tempest lasting a
mere hour, the people of the moholla became aware of his
special status. Within an hour that day, the army entered
every house, and seven people were killed in the moholla,
while three women were raped. Although the residents of
the moholla found out very soon the names of the seven
men who were killed, nobody knew the names of the three
women who were raped; they couldn't identify them; for
that matter, they didn't even know whether they were
children, or young or old women. That was because the
servant of Moulana Bodu's household, from whom the
moholla's stupefied people got the news, couldn't provide
the names of the three women. As seven corpses lay in the
moholla and the people were full of anxiety over the
impending curfew, the servant told them that he had heard
from some soldiers that three of them had sexual intercourse
with three women. The people of the moholla looked
blankly as they listened to him and then gazed back at the
corpses. They did a count of their family members; there
was one person short in five families, while there were two
people short in Khwaja Ahmed Ali's family. The people of
the moholla found out that, as soon as the army entered
Khwaja Ahmed Ali's house, they shot his elder son,

Khwaja Shofiq, dead. Both father and son were then standing in the compound of the house. When, in front of the father's eyes, and for no reason at all, Khwaja Shofiq's lifeless body slumped to the ground, he rushed up the stairs to the rooftop and called out the azan. All the residents of the moholla later recalled that, yes, they had heard the melodious azan. At that tempestuous moment, when daylight was like a sable-coloured liquid, and the sphere of sound was fragmented into thousands of pieces as if a mountain had been crushed down, they had heard the echoes of the azan wafting over the rooftops of Lakshmi Bazar's houses with their peeling plaster. And after they learnt that Khwaja Ahmed Ali was the muezzin at that stormy moment, all of them recalled that when they heard the azan, they had recognized his voice. All of them concurred that they had never heard the azan recited so mellifluously before, and that they had thought that only the voice of Belal could be like this. They also recalled that he completed the azan, and that in the last stanza of the azan, he uttered 'Allahu Akbar' four times instead of two. But when the people of the moholla went up to Khwaja Ahmed Ali's roof and saw his dead body lying face down and then found out that he had been shot while he was reciting the azan, they could not accept it. They recalled that, at the end of the azan, he had declared to everyone in the moholla, four times over, that only Allah was great. They were confused, and this confusion of theirs persisted all their lives. They turned over Khwaja Ahmed Ali's dead body and noticed drops of blood on his white beard. They then brought his body down and placed it beside Khwaja Shofiq's body in the courtyard. That day, they retrieved a total of seven corpses from the streets and houses of the moholla. All the dead people were male, and the age of the youngest boy among them was thirteen, and that of the oldest man, eighty. Except for two of them, all the others had been picked up from the earth, as if they were trees which had once stood upright in the courtyard with their branches and leaves spread out but had been felled in a gale and were now being moved. One of the other two, Khwaja Ahmed Ali, was found on the roof, and Altaf Hussain, of House No. 64, was floating in the well. The people of the moholla couldn't, at first, figure out whether he had fallen into the water after being shot or whether he had been shot after jumping into the well. After pulling out the body using a rope and a hook, they became confused when they tried to find a bullet wound. They couldn't find any sign of a bullet wound and they inferred that perhaps he had drowned in the well. But the people of the moholla recalled that, afterwards, they had looked closely at the water in the well and noticed that it was blood red, and so they examined Altaf Hussain again and discovered a small wound in the crown of his head, hidden under his hair. But they couldn't find the point of exit of the bullet; they were certain that Altaf Hussain's body had not allowed the bullet that took his life to exit. The people of the moholla couldn't say what Altaf Hussain gained from this; they only said, *'Guli dhukchhe, kintu bairoya parenaika.* The bullet went in, but it couldn't come out.' And seeing the bullet wound in the middle of his crown they were certain that he had been shot and killed after he jumped into the well. The people of the moholla brought all the dead bodies to Khwaja Ahmed Ali's courtyard and laid them together, and not being able to go anywhere on account of the curfew, they sat there with the corpses. They were bewildered; there was no outpouring of grief. That day, the people of Lakshmi Bazar sat silently with the seven corpses; the streets of Lakshmi Bazar were as silent as death, there wasn't a single dog on the streets, there wasn't a single owl in the sky that flapped its wings noisily and flew by. They felt as if they had not heard a single sound since the beginning of creation. But after that, as the night advanced, they realized that they could hear a woman crying. It was as if, from the depths of forgetfulness, they had once again become aware of this vocal expression of humanity; but they saw that nobody in their group was weeping. So, they strained their ears and listened to the sound of an unknown woman crying, and gradually it occurred to them that they had heard this sound of crying even before the soldiers left. The people of the moholla felt certain, then, that another body lay somewhere, in some household, with whom, for some reason, others had not been in contact. They then awakened their numbed senses and listened and realized that the sound of crying was emanating from the direction of Moulana Bodu's house. It was in Moulana Bodu's house that someone had been crying for a long time, and when this truth was established, the people of the moholla were initially in disbelief, but after that they began to feel delight even in their grief. Because earlier that day, the people of the moholla had seen Moulana Bodu all by himself, in a different light. With a band of people dressed in khaki garb, Moulana Bodu, clad in a grey-coloured poplin jobba, had carried out a veritable slaughter in the streets, houses, courtyards, well-sides, and roofs of Lakshmi Bazar. But now, with this sound of crying, the anger and delight of the people of the moholla became one and reached such heights, they felt that unless they saw for themselves this woman from Moulana Bodu's family weeping, this grief of theirs wouldn't end, their delight wouldn't be complete. The people of the moholla then went to Moulana Bodu's residence, and after going there they realized their error. They found out that, first of all, the one who was crying was not a woman at all; it was Moulana Bodu's younger son, Abul Bashar. He was crying because the Pakistani soldiers had shot and killed his beloved dog, Bhulu. The people of the moholla saw the servants of the household sitting surrounding the reddish-brown-coloured Bhulu under the electric light in Moulana Bodu's courtyard. They found out that after Bhulu had been killed for whatever reason, when

Abul Bashar wouldn't stop crying, Moulana Bodu had pressed his hand on his son's mouth and then the leader of the soldiers, a Punjabi captain, had told Moulana Bodu to let the boy be. He had said, *'Unko rone do.* Let him cry.' At the very time the people of Lakshmi Bazar were hiding under the cover of the silent night, with dead bodies left behind in their homes, the Pakistani soldiers had accorded this special deference to Moulana Bodu – his son got the opportunity to express his grief for his beloved dog that was now dead. He had begun to weep even before the soldiers left the moholla. But the people of the moholla waited the whole night, bearing their grief for those killed; they waited a whole year, until the moment when, on a Thursday in late autumn, a band of freedom fighters clad in olive-green uniforms arrived in the moholla with Sten guns in their hand, and long, bushy beards on their faces. They declared, *'Aar bhoy nai, shalara khotom.* There's no more cause for fear, the bastards are finished.' The people of the moholla came out into the street and kept patting the shoulders of the wild-looking men. Then, Abul Kashem's son, Joshim, came running, holding a flag with a red sun and a golden map painted on deep green, and shouted out, 'Joy Bangla!' and then Alauddin's Ma, having come out to see the freedom fighters, collapsed on the earth and wept, *'Awra amar Alauddinre maira phalaichhe.* They killed my Alauddin.' The freedom fighter boys didn't pick up this woman who had collapsed on the ground; they didn't console her, they didn't even look at her; they merely surrounded the grieving woman. There were rifles slung on all of their backs, and cartridge cases on the belts tied at their waists. They stood indifferently; they undid the knots in their long hair with their thin, dirty fingers, they puffed cigarettes. Lying on the earth inside their circle, Alauddin's Ma wept. Among all the people there, the news of the arrival of the freedom fighters in the moholla was of special interest to three women; they stood on the street, and together with the rest of the people, they gazed at the boys with unkempt hair and dirty clothes. After that, when they advanced and told the indifferent youths about their own sons and wanted to know about them, these wild-looking, bearded youths surrounded them, and in the way a father embraces his daughter, they placed their hands on their shoulders and assured them that their sons would definitely return. But this didn't prove to be entirely true; Babul and Alamgir came back, but Mohammad Selim didn't. All his Ma's hopes were belied; her son didn't return at the end of the Liberation War. She had realized he wouldn't return, but she still nurtured the same old fond hopes. The people of the moholla said that Mohammad Selim's Ma was waiting for him, as was Mayarani Malakar. But Abdul Mojid knew that Mayarani was not waiting for Mohammad Selim, although he didn't know who Mayarani was waiting for and why she remained unmarried all these years. When it was evident that there was no possibility of Mohammad Selim returning after the war, and the trunk with his personal belongings was broken – Abdul Mojid knew for a fact that the single note written by Mayarani that was found inside hadn't been written by her. It was only Abdul Mojid who knew the unfortunate fact that the letter, consisting of a single line, that Mohammad Selim had received in response to his twenty-one love letters, had actually not been written by Mayarani. When Abdul Mojid was not immersed in family matters, he could hear Mayarani worshipping God Shani on Saturday evenings. Her melancholy voice came wafting from the next house, from across the wall, like a Baul song whose meaning he couldn't fathom. On Saturday evenings, Mayarani chanted like a dirge, *'Ashen, Shoni, boshen khate, possad debo haate haate.* Come, Shani, sit on the cot, I'll feed you the sacred offering with my own hand.' Abdul Mojid didn't understand why Mayarani invited God Shani, but he sensed that she felt no joy in this perpetual solicitation, there was only sorrow in her voice. Abdul Mojid remembered that Mayarani's Ma's voice did not have the same hypnotic tinge of sorrow. At that time – he still wore shorts then – on Saturday evenings, he used to climb over and sit atop the wall between the two houses. Mayarani's Ma used to come out then, with a ghomta drawn over her head and a dot of sindoor, large and round like the full moon, on her forehead. Mayarani's Ma used to come with a lamp lit with mustard oil held on a bell-metal platter, sit beside the tulsi plant near the gate, and invite

God Shani in the same way. The lamp kept on the low pedestal erected at the base of the tulsi plant used to be lit, and Abdul Mojid used to hear Mayarani's Ma's invocation of God Shani – *'Ashen, Shoni, boshen khate, possad debo haate haate.* Come, Shani, sit on the cot, I'll feed you the sacred offering with my own hand.' Once the worship was completed in this way, Mayarani used to bring a large bowl and place a single lump of chira soaked in milk with mashed bananas in the outstretched palms of the boys and girls waiting in the compound, including Abdul Mojid sitting on the wall. Even today, Abdul Mojid sometimes thought that if he only stretched out his hand, the dark-skinned and silly-looking Mayarani would place the prasad in it in the same way. Abdul Mojid could not make out why Mohammad Selim had been enchanted by this dark-skinned girl, but it had occurred to him that, given Mohammad Selim's lively exuberance, it was certainly possible for him to fall in love with her, and then go off to war forsaking that love. Mayarani was then in Banglabazar School, preparing to take the matric examination for the third time after having failed twice, and that was when Mohammad Selim was struck by Cupid's flowery arrow and got derailed. The people of the moholla had observed Mohammad Selim's abnormal behaviour for a few days; they had noticed that when Mayarani came out on the street, Mohammad Selim followed her slowly in a zigzag on his cycle or stood with neatly combed and parted hair at the street corner, mouth agape. They had also noticed that Mayarani paid no attention to Mohammad Selim's excitement; she used to walk on, holding a book pressed to her bosom and looking ahead. But even before the people of the moholla could be exasperated by Mohammad Selim's love affliction, they observed that his passion had waned. Actually, Mohammad Selim had then discovered the fact that, every Saturday, Abdul Mojid consumed the prasad of milk and banana given to him by Mayarani with her own hands, and so he altered his way of wooing her. His persistence was hidden from people's sight. Mohammad Selim called Abdul Mojid, and as he opened the jars in his father's confectionery store and filled the boy's hands with laddus and biscuits, he said, 'Law, kha. Here, eat.' Abdul Mojid then thought that he had been a dunderhead to eat the laddus and biscuits, because the very next day Mohammad Selim gave him a letter to deliver to Mayarani. Once again, like a dunderhead, Abdul Mojid took it to Mayarani and when, standing under their flowering shefali tree, Mayarani refused to accept it, Abdul Mojid took the letter to his house and hid it in a niche in a wall of his room. In this way, twenty-one letters had accumulated in the niche in the wall of Abdul Mojid's house by the time war broke out, just before Mohammad Selim had his final higher secondary school examinations and went away to war leaving Mayarani behind. Abdul Mojid subsequently used to think that Mohammad Selim ought to have

received love, and that Mayarani ought to have given him
at least that much; because after all, he was like one of those
men who had arrived one day in the moholla, battle-
fatigued and with the smell of gunpowder on them, the day
Alauddin's Ma had finally, after such a long time, collapsed
in the dust and wept uncontrollably. But the day Alauddin's
body was laid with the six other bodies on old reed mats in
Khwaja Ahmed Ali's courtyard, his Ma had sat silently, like
a terrified, stupefied creature. That day, it was only Abul
Bashar from the moholla who had wept. The people of the
moholla recall that, once they heard that sound of weeping,
it seemed to them that Abul Bashar's cries could be heard
all through the night. Everyone in the moholla knew that
this boy was Moulana Bodu's favourite child. That was why
he conceded to his son's wish to keep an impure creature
as a pet, and as a result, when permission was granted to
grieve for the dog, he was overwhelmed with emotion, for
his son, his son's dog, and the Pakistani captain. But
because of all the turmoil of 1971, as events transpired,
Moulana Bodu lost this son of his; he did not suffer any
other major loss. Other than this one death, he was able to
see his family through the difficult times he faced in
connection with Bangladesh becoming independent, and
in the year 1980, he became a major leader of the same
political party he had belonged to. Abdul Mojid now
observed that Moulana Bodu's party, together with Ajij
Pathan's, was jointly protesting against the government.

Abdul Mojid heard Moulana Bodu and his sons address the people of the moholla as 'bhaishob', or 'brothers', and invite them to participate in the struggle. Hearing that, the strap on Abdul Mojid's sandal went *phot* and snapped; he saw crows flying out from inside the long jobba of Moulana Bodu's son. Returning home, as he stood gazing at his wife's face, he could not forget about his dead sister; there was a bayonet wound near her shoulder and a mess of cuts and bruises below her breasts, and when the nation was close to the final stage of the process of freedom, she lay on a field in Rayer Bazar, staring at the sky with unmoving eyes. Abdul Mojid couldn't forget about all that Moulana Bodu had done, because he couldn't forget about Momena. After being subject to the message of thanks delivered over the mic by Moulana Bodu's son on Nawabpur Road, he returned home and kept gazing at Yasmin's face, and then within the moholla, once again, the sound of a mic grew louder. This man too addressed them as 'bhaishob' and thanked them for making the strike successful. He concluded the announcement exclaiming, 'Joy Bangla!' and after that, he began once again, saying 'bhaishob.' The people of the moholla were puzzled. Perhaps they remembered for no reason at all that the day Moulana Bodu, with a black-checked scarf thrown over his shoulders, came forward and stood facing the captain of the Pakistani army, Ajij Pathan wasn't present in the moholla. And when Ajij Pathan returned to the moholla with his family around

the end of December that year, Moulana Bodu wasn't
there. The people of the moholla remembered that the day
the Pakistani army first arrived there, Moulana Bodu took
them to Ajij Pathan's house. The soldiers set fire to it. One
soldier, swore, 'Bastard!' and sprayed a round of bullets at
the arch made of a boat's hull at the gate of the house; after
that, it was set on fire along with the house. People couldn't
remember when Ajij Pathan left the moholla; they only
remembered that, some day after the 25th of March,
Moulana Bodu arrived there with a gang of people. They
broke the locks on the houses of the Hindus in the moholla
and looted them. They broke the lock on Ajij Pathan's
house and carried all his belongings to Moulana Bodu's.
They used crowbars to remove the old doors and windows
of these looted houses as well as their frames. After that,
the day the Pakistani army set fire to Ajij Pathan's house,
it didn't burn; only the bullet-ridden boat with its broken
prow and stern blazed furiously. The people of the moholla
were aware of the fact that Moulana Bodu wanted to make
all of Ajij Pathan's property his own. But subsequently,
events transpired in such a manner that the people of the
moholla surmised that Moulana Bodu had merely assumed
responsibility for Ajij Pathan's property. When Ajij Pathan
returned on the 30th of December, the last Thursday of
1971, the people of the moholla were overjoyed. Before the
tall Ajij Pathan, dressed in white pyjama-punjabi, entered
his house, he walked slowly, like a victorious general, along

the streets of Lakshmi Bazar. Seeing him, even the womenfolk who had lost their sons and husbands hurrahed. Ajij Pathan entered the courtyard of every house in the moholla, embraced every person there; after that, he offered prayers at the graves of Khwaja Ahmed Ali and his son, and then went to his own house. With the doors and window frames removed, the scorched house looked like a skull. Standing at the door, he raised his head and looked at the devastated house, then turned towards the people who had followed him and were waiting silently. The people did not discern any grief or sadness on his face. When he waved his hand towards the public as if it were a flag, they wanted to rise up like a rogue wave. He then said, with a pleasant smile, *'Amago onek kichhu daeown lagchhe, tobu amra shwadhin hoichhi.* We had to sacrifice a lot, but still we've become independent.' After Ajij Pathan entered his house, the people of the moholla broke the door of Moulana Bodu's house, brought out all the things and piled them up in Ajij Pathan's courtyard. Examining the various items, Ajij Pathan's wife said they were all theirs, except for two items of clothing. The people of the moholla were pleased to hear that, and after some time, everyone went back to their respective homes. A few days later, observing, first, Moulana Bodu's looted, abandoned family homestead, and then, a wooden boat under construction once again in front of Ajij Pathan's house, the crisis in the heart of the boy Abdul Mojid which had set in after Moulana Bodu swore at Momena, slipped away, unbeknownst to him. He returned home and reassured his mother, *'Ajij Pathaner bashar gatey eikga notun nao banaibar lagchhe.* They've started building a new boat at the gate of Ajij Pathan's house.' But in the beginning of 1972, the people of the moholla and Abdul Mojid didn't realize that the matter hadn't yet been resolved, and that they were to see a lot more. They didn't imagine that within two years, even before the boat constructed at Ajij Pathan's gate could become rundown and useless, Moulana Bodu would return to the moholla and would, at first, slink through the streets like a shadow, and after that, in 1980, some of them, including Abdul Mojid, would see Moulana Bodu felicitating his anointed successor, or Emir. Or that, standing in front of the water tower at the Kolta Bazar crossing, Abdul Mojid would hear Moulana Bodu delivering a speech. That day, the people of the moholla would learn from this speech how Moulana Bodu's beloved son died following independence while they were in flight. The people of the moholla could now recall that, on that day, while delivering his speech, raising and holding his arms high in the direction of the sky, Moulana Bodu had said that that had been a test. In the same way that Allah had tested Prophet Ibrahim by asking him to sacrifice his favourite son, he had been tested in his life and thus lost his beloved son. In 1973, after Moulana Bodu returned, the people of the moholla came to know that Abul Bashar had died; and although they didn't know about the cause of death until Moulana Bodu delivered his speech in 1980, they thought that this was a sort of revenge. Later, the day Moulana Bodu elaborated upon the subject of Prophet Ibrahim and his test, those from the moholla who were listening to his speech came to know that Abul Bashar had drowned in a pond while they were hiding in a village in Khepupara. One issue that the people of the moholla were unanimous about was that Abul Bashar was indeed beloved by Moulana Bodu. In this regard, the residents of the moholla had a theory, which was that this boy had a kind of disability and that was why his father had a special weakness for him. Although the suspicion of the people of the moholla regarding Abul Bashar's disability was subsequently proven true, they hadn't been certain initially. They said that Abul Bashar was neither a boy nor a girl. No one could say how this notion originated, and once the word spread, although they had their suspicions, they couldn't be certain. From the time this son of his was born, Moulana Bodu kept him in his in-laws' house in Demra, and when he first set foot in the moholla, he was a six-year-old boy and the people of the moholla saw that he was always kept fully clothed. The matter was in no way of any significance as far as the people of the moholla were concerned, but nonetheless, they were able to know definitively about the matter when the razakar, Abdul Goni, was caught in Jinjira on the 21st of December. Abdul Goni was brought to Lakshmi Bazar that very afternoon by two freedom fighters, and people got to know from him how all that had happened in the country as well as in the moholla had actually transpired. First of all, besides the people killed in the moholla during the nine months, the people of the moholla also had a list of eight missing people. It was later learnt that three people had left home and joined the Liberation War; they still needed to know about the other five. Just before noon, Abdul Goni was brought to St Gregory's School and tied with a rope to a post inside the compound. He refused to speak. Seeing his appearance and the look on his face, the public was reminded of a cornered fox. He was then taken to Victoria Park and was laid, face down, on a concrete bench there. He was laid in such a way that his head stuck out. After that, he was tied to the bench with a rope; a low table was kept beneath his face, and a microphone was placed on it, as were three long lists of names, and a bottle of Vita Cola with a straw that was within reach of his mouth. After that, his lungi was lifted up and the muzzle of a freedom fighter's SLR was shoved in. People from all directions then gathered at the steps and dais of the memorial pillar to martyred soldiers and in the expanse of green grass below that. They couldn't figure out whether or not the barrel of the SLR had been inserted into Abdul Goni's anus. A group of them thought it had. But another group was certain that it had not, because when Abdul Goni moved, the weapon sticking out from under the lungi didn't move.

They said that the nose of the barrel had merely been pushed into his groin. But their dispute was cut short just then, because Abdul Goni's voice came floating out from the loudspeakers. It took Abdul Goni more than two hours to finish going through the three lists. While reading out the names on the list, he identified some of them, but was unable to identify the others. When his voice floated out from the loudspeakers, the public surrounding him were petrified as they heard him speak about the days they had emerged from, as if from a nightmare; but now it appeared to them that everything they were hearing was new, or that they knew nothing earlier. As Abdul Goni was identifying a particular name and elaborating upon the fate he or she met, a man or a woman or someone who might be the husband, son, friend, or neighbour of the missing person would begin to wail out from the assembly. When Abdul Goni finished speaking in Victoria Park, twenty-one women threw themselves to the ground and wailed, ten men and boys sobbed, and the entire public was overcome with emotion. The people of Lakshmi Bazar heard from Abdul Goni that when Abu Korim's elder son was returning home, he was picked up from near the food godown in Kolta Bazar after dusk and taken to the military camp where he was butchered at night. The people of Lakshmi Bazar heard from Abdul Goni about the death of Ismail, the hajam of Malitola. Although Ismail the hajam's name was not on the list of people missing from Lakshmi

Bazar, they remembered his name then. On a Tuesday in the month of June, with his head bent down, he had been sharpening a razor on a whetstone after sprinkling some water on it in the courtyard of Moulana Bodu's house, under the disinterested, murky gaze of the people of the moholla. Moulana Bodu's house had been decorated with coloured paper that day, and seeing that, the people of the moholla had thought that Moulana Bodu was surely getting married again. Their notion was, of course, dispelled once Moulana Bodu invited them, and when, unable to turn down the invitation, they presented themselves at Moulana Bodu's house, they spotted Ismail the hajam sitting in the shade of the custard apple tree in the courtyard. They saw him sitting with a piece of wood stuck under his heels, whetting a razor single-mindedly and checking the sharpness of the blade by touching its gleaming edge with his thumb. It was only then they found out that Moulana Bodu's son, Abul Bashar, was to be circumcised; because when Moulana Bodu's servant invited them, he had only said, 'Moulana shabe apnere dupure jaite koise. Moulana saab has asked you to come in the afternoon.' Learning about it now, the people of the moholla burst out laughing, and their gossip-fed suspicions about the absence of the boy's male organ were allayed. They remained seated on the foldable chairs brought from the decorator's shop, but they didn't see anyone else there attending to the guests; there were only the household servants, and Ismail the hajam sitting under the custard apple tree. It looked like Ismail the hajam had been sharpening the razor for an eternity, but apparently it wasn't sharp enough to satisfy his thumb; he once again began rubbing the razor, one side after the other, against the whetstone, all the while testing it with his thumb. Just as the people of the moholla became drowsy at the sound of Ismail the hajam sharpening the razor, their weary eyes observed Moulana Bodu bringing Abul Bashar. He was made to sit on an alpona-adorned mat, bathed in water mixed with rose water, and then taken inside, even as Ismail the hajam kept whetting the razor. Although the people of the moholla found this monotonous conduct of his annoying, nonetheless they praised him, saying, the way he was sharpening the blade of the razor, the foreskin would be snipped off before either the blade or the boy's penis knew it. After a while, Ismail the hajam ran his thumb over the blade of the razor for a final time, put the razor carefully into its case, folded a clean white rag to turn it into a thick wick; then he burnt it to ashes over a flame, and placed the ashes on a piece of banana leaf. The people observed the meticulousness of Ismail the hajam's work. After preparing the blade for excising the foreskin of the penis, and a bandage of ash to wrap around the wound, he went inside the house with all his instruments, accompanied by the *flip-flop* sound of his rubber slippers. The people of the moholla didn't see anything more after that. There was nobody from the moholla inside the room where the main task of the khatna or circumcision was carried out, and at that time the door of that windowless room was shut. The people of the moholla could have left then, because they were already suffering the heat and were thirsty and hungry, and there was nothing before them but the vacant courtyard. But they were unable to say why they didn't do that and chose to wait instead. Actually, even if they couldn't see what was happening inside the closed room, it was as if all of them could actually see it. Because all of them had once had their penises circumcised in the same way. They imagined Abul Bashar's clothes being removed, and thus the boy's fair-skinned buttocks were exposed before their eyes. He was then made to sit on a wooden floor seat, and his father wound his arms around the boy's arms and legs firmly from behind and lifted up his exposed groin in front of the hajam. They could then imagine Ismail the hajam once again, now squatting in front of the boy and working swiftly. It occurred to them that Ismail the hajam's hands moved so fast that the boy didn't even get the chance to utter a moan, as if the hajam's blade snipped off the boy's foreskin in an instant, like the soft peel of an onion, and in that very instant they heard the boy's screams. And it was as if, the very next moment, they saw the hajam standing with the razor in his hand, drops of blood trickling down the blade, and it occurred to them that the thirst that Ismail the hajam had awakened in the blade had been quenched. Now, after visualizing everything, the people of the moholla smiled. Just then, Ismail the hajam emerged from the room; he didn't say anything to those present, he didn't look at anyone either, but they gathered that Moulana Bodu's younger son's khatna was over. After that, they went back to their respective homes, and on the way back it struck them that, besides inviting them and making them sit in the courtyard, Moulana Bodu had not offered them even a glass of sherbet. They forgot about the matter thereafter, and until six months and ten days after that, when Abdul Goni, with his face down, uttered Ismail the hajam's name over the mic, they didn't feel the need or have the time to remember it. But hearing Abdul Goni, they realized that Moulana Bodu had called them to his house and made them sit there only so that they could see Ismail the hajam sharpening his razor. Because they got to know that, on that day, Ismail the hajam didn't circumcise Abul Bashar, and even before the next day could dawn, he was killed. He was called out of his residence in Malitola that very night, taken to the military camp, and butchered. The people of Lakshmi Bazar found out that six months and ten days earlier, on that sweltering hot afternoon of June, Ismail the hajam didn't have to snip Abul Bashar's foreskin. He was merely taken inside and made to sit there, and after some time he was shown out of the room and told to keep his mouth shut. Ismail the hajam didn't open his mouth; the people of the moholla recalled that Ismail the hajam's clenched jaws had seemed hard as stone and that he had

proceeded towards the shade of the custard apple tree
without looking at anyone sitting in the courtyard. But,
everyone realized now, Ismail had been angry. Maybe it
was not possible for him to simply terminate the extreme
patience and devotion with which he had whetted the razor,
and maybe he thought that if he was unable to express
himself in some way it would not be possible for him to
continue living. Now, standing at Victoria Park, the people
of the moholla heard from Abdul Goni that, after arriving
at the beguiling green shade of the custard apple tree, the
control that Ismail the hajam had exercised over himself so
far slackened, and while he was packing his things in the
tin valise, he had muttered something faintly. As if talking
to himself, he had uttered a sentence, the sentence that the
people of the moholla now heard from Abdul Goni's
mouth: *'Halar hijrar abar musolmani!* A circumcision for
the bastard's hijra!' At that moment, there was only a single
person within audible range, and unfortunately that person
was Abdul Goni. He was standing right there, clad in a
lungi and vest, and Malitola's Ismail couldn't recognize
him. Maybe the chlorophyll from the green shade of the
custard apple tree had confounded his senses at that
moment, or maybe he really didn't know Abdul Goni.
Abdul Goni said that when Ismail the hajam muttered that,
he hadn't understood what he meant. Because he didn't
know what it was about. However, as a vigilant razakar of
this country that was swarming with enemies, he kept

Moulana Bodu informed at all times, even about the speed and direction of the wind. That's why he thought fit to inform Moulana Bodu about what Ismail the hajam had muttered to himself. Hearing what Abdul Goni said, Moulana Bodu was at first perturbed; he warned him icily so that this denigration and slander did not travel from him to another ear, and after that, as a result of what he then said, standing in the veranda of his house with his gloomy eyes fixed on a small rectangular slice of sky, that night, Ismail the hajam saw a man waiting in the semi-dark room of the primary school with a knife in his hand. When he sighted, amidst that darkness, the lustre of this instrument of slaughter, he realized that the metal blade of this weapon had been sharpened with much devotion, and that both this eager weapon as well as the weapon bearer would not be satisfied without the taste of blood. The people heard from Abdul Goni that thanks to the practical wisdom Ismail the hajam had developed – notwithstanding his apparent ignorance – through lifelong cohabitation with the metallic nature of the snipping tool, when he spotted the butcher's waiting knife, he knew he had reached the end of his life, a life of hatred, love, suffering and rare moments of joy. At the time of his murder, he surrendered himself to the cold, cement floor without the three razakars having to exert any force. The public present at Victoria Park discovered to their astonishment from Abdul Goni's testimony that, in his final moments, Ismail the hajam was like a bemused adventurer. The way Tenzing Norgay might have said, after venturing through sun and blizzard, climbing 29,028 feet and planting a final foot down on the summit of Mt Everest, 'So this is Everest,' it was learnt from Abdul Goni that, in the same way, Ismail the hajam placed his head under the blade and said, just once, *'Ayamne eita shyash hoilo.* So this is how it ends.' Counting Ismail the hajam, Abdul Goni was able to identify twenty-one people from the three lists of names, and he said that all of them were dead. The grieving and enraged people heard from him that each one of them was butchered and the heads were severed from the bodies, and the headless torsos were taken at night by rickshaw-van and thrown into the Buriganga river, while the severed heads were buried outside the Christian cemetery. Then, after hearing his testimony, the people of Lakshmi Bazar, the people of Nayabazar and Siddique Bazar, and the people of Patuatuli and Narinda evacuated the Victoria Park square and moved towards the Christian cemetery. Those who weren't present in the gathering at Victoria Park or were unable to be there, saw in that dead afternoon of winter, on that third day of the month of Zilqad, that, just like on the day of Ashura in the month of Mohorrom, a silent and grieving public moved along Narinda, or through Padmanidhi Lane, or went around the Rathkhola crossing, and walked down Tipu Sultan Road; they moved in the direction of the Christian cemetery in the northeast. They dug and found fifty-six skulls outside the cemetery wall, beside the railway line, but they could not extricate the twenty-one belonging to those named by Abdul Goni from among those. They washed the skulls in water and made them spotlessly clean and laid them on banana leaves spread out on the earth in seven rows, and at the time it occurred to them that it was as if a magnificent jamdani sari had been created over the green earth through the combined efforts of nature and the human skulls. In that afternoon laden with melancholy, seeing the skulls arrayed over banana leaves, the people of the moholla had imagined an exquisitely woven jamdani sari, and now, it was in that jamdani sari that they saw their mothers and lovers, their daughters and daughters' daughters attired whenever they gathered during the various festivals of life. That day, the people of Lakshmi Bazar had realized that their five missing members, whom Abdul Goni had identified as having been killed, couldn't be distinguished from the rest, just like they couldn't identify the three women on the day the Pakistani army first arrived in the moholla. On that day too, after the soldiers left, when the people of the moholla were reeling from the shock of discovering the seven bodies and from the fact that they themselves were even alive, and were overcome by a sense of lassitude, they had seen the sad and sullen look of humiliation on the faces of their womenfolk. For each boy and girl, man and woman of the moholla, it was like the first initiation to the knowledge that there existed

something in this wide world called rape. The sight that
they had witnessed all their lives and not realized the
meaning of – that of a rooster chasing a hen – once the
soldiers arrived in the moholla, they thought that, right in
front of their eyes, their mothers, young daughters, and
intimately beloved wives were running helter-skelter, like
terrified hens in a courtyard, for fear of their lives and to
escape sexual assault. They became aware of that so heart-
rendingly that they were numb to any sense other than
sorrow. They felt helpless. Because they had imagined that
only a hen feared falling victim to rape, as did primitive,
cave-dwelling women. But now, in a single hour, the
Pakistani army had torn to shreds the raiment of civilization
woven by humanity over fifty thousand years, and the
people of Lakshmi Bazar witnessed man's primitiveness
once again, in their own moholla, with a tragic helplessness;
mother and son together, and father and young daughter,
became aware of the meaning of rape. At that time, the boy
Abdul Mojid had looked at his young sister's face. The
soldiers had left then, and like the weary branches of a tree
after a frenzied storm, they stood immobile, and then, for
some reason, Abdul Mojid looked at Momena's face. It
could be said that perhaps he wasn't looking for anything
on his sister's face, and wasn't thinking about anything in
particular either, nothing other than the thought that the
soldiers had left; despite that, he had seen a dark gloom on
his Momena Aapa's face, and Momena had realized that

Abdul Mojid was observing her gloom. Or it may also be that Abdul Mojid wasn't even observing Momena's gloom, maybe he had merely cast his eyes in that direction and not engaged his sight; nonetheless, Momena had scolded him, '*Ki dekhoch tui baare baare!* What are you gaping at!' At that dark moment, Abdul Mojid had remembered another day tinged with greater darkness, when Momena had exclaimed in the same way, '*Ki dekhoch tui!* What are you looking at!' On the 2nd of April 1971, a Friday, when they had taken shelter on the first floor of a stranger's house in Jinjira after being chased by the Pakistani army and were sitting there with countless others, his eyes had fallen on his elderly Ma, on Momena's terrified, perspiring face, and on his two weeping little sisters. Abdul Mojid hadn't observed anything when he looked at his Ma, two younger sisters and Momena Aapa. Actually, he now thought that he hadn't got around to looking at his sister at all in those nine months, and when he did, in fact, first look at her, there was a wound on her throat, like a brown hibiscus, and her face was slanted, her eyes gazing at infinity. The boy Abdul Mojid was sitting on his knees beside her, with his arms crossed over his chest and his eyes fixed on hers. But she didn't ask him then, 'What are you gaping at?' the way she did in that room in Jinjira. Abdul Mojid had not taken amiss Momena's rebuke in the room in Jinjira, or maybe he had not heard her properly then. After he, his Ma and his three sisters had fled through fields, roads and abandoned

Hindu houses and found shelter in this house, and sat on the floor of a room on the first floor along with a crowd of people who, like them, had fled, Abdul Mojid had then felt as if his senses had departed his being and that his mind was no longer in control of his body. During those moments of overwhelmed bewilderment, he saw that his arms were no longer functional, they hung down limply from his shoulders like a useless burden, and he realized that his pyjamas were getting wet around the thigh, but he was completely unable to stop it. Now Abdul Mojid recalled that, at that time, he was in a perilous third dimension between consciousness and unconsciousness, helplessly witnessing his own limbs becoming independent of his control. He had then gazed helplessly at his Ma's and sister's faces, and then Momena had asked him, 'What are you looking at?' After that, when Abdul Mojid's bodily fluids kept on streaming out, disregarding all his fears and despair, his sister's grace became manifest to the overwhelmed boy. Momena covered his shame, and using the anchal of her sari, she wiped Abdul Mojid's urine from the floor. After that, Abdul Mojid sensed the return of the concordance between his body and mind that had been severed, and emerging from his state of bewilderment, he buried his face between his knees and sobbed. His elderly mother, who was sitting silently like a terrified creature, realized her son was still a child, and she pulled his head and placed it on her bosom, she kissed his head; she said,

'*Baap, baap amar!* O my dearest child!' But except on that day, the unmanliness of the boy Abdul Mojid didn't ever get a chance to manifest itself. In fact, when on the morning of the 26th of March, sunlight emerged and they opened the door and stood in the light of that first day of war, then, looking at his Ma and sisters, unbeknownst to Abdul Mojid, the sense was born inside him, which is born at some point inside every man, that he was responsible for these people. Stepping out into the street of the moholla, he saw that each and every person had been disoriented by terror, and he felt the stillness that lay congealed everywhere. He then left the moholla and secretly walked all the way to Victoria Park. He saw smoke billowing from the direction of Nayabazar, he got the smell of burning coal. Returning home, he looked at his Ma and elder sister and he saw in them the same suppressed fear that he had observed in the people of the moholla. He could clearly feel a mute terror within himself too, but before dawn on the 25th of March, when they were woken up by the sound of gunfire and uproar and fell into confusion and saw the country burning in blazing flames, then Abdul Mojid had to say, '*Dorayo na.* Don't be afraid.' The next day, they witnessed in a disturbed state of mind that the people of the moholla were disregarding the curfew and fleeing. The Hindus left first, furtively, leaving their homes unguarded, while the Muslims followed close behind. The sound of crickets chirping could be heard on the silent, still streets

of the moholla by late afternoon. Abdul Mojid's Ma
became even more perturbed once the moholla turned
desolate, and he too felt that they couldn't stay all alone like
this in the moholla. Yet they remained, because they
couldn't decide where they would go after leaving home,
and since their next-door neighbour, Rahim Byapari, had
said that he too wouldn't leave. But when Rahim Byapari
locked his door and left with his family the very next
day, Abdul Mojid's Ma broke down. Caught in that
situation, Abdul Mojid took his family to Jinjira, and after
just a single night, as if after a nightmare, he returned once
more to the moholla, holding his Ma's and sisters' hands,
and upon unlocking the door and entering the room, they
felt an amazing sense of safety, and said that they would
not leave home again. But subsequently they realized that
it was no longer safe inside the house either, and
consequently one day, the boy Abdul Mojid had to search
for, discover and carry Momena's corpse home. The day
Rahim Byapari left home and Abdul Mojid's Ma became
restless, Abdul Mojid felt as if he was a sailor looking
frantically for a lighthouse in an unfathomable sea. At first,
he thought they could go to his aunt's house in the village
in Cumilla, but he realized at once that they wouldn't be
able to go so far. After that, he remembered Anwar, and
he decided that he would go across the river with his Ma
and sisters and take them to Anwar's house. On the
afternoon of the 1st of April, they hurriedly packed some

things and set out. The desolate street of the moholla seemed like some vast wilderness to them, where day had perhaps turned to night. Sticking to the edge of the road and advancing like silent shadows, they made their way from the moholla to Victoria Park and got into a rickshaw. There was no curfew for that bit of time, and they skirted the field at Armanitola and arrived in front of the jailhouse. When they reached the jailhouse and saw all around them the pointing muzzles of machine guns and soldiers in khaki uniform in sandbag bunkers, their sense of isolation grew. Abdul Mojid held his breath, but his Ma couldn't contain her terror any longer; she kept reciting the kolema loudly, *'La Ilaha Ilallahu Muhammadur Rasulullah.'* In this way, the rickshaw took them and proceeded along Chawk Circular Road and through the narrow lane at Champatoli, dropping them finally at Sowari Ghat, on the bank of the Buriganga. When they set foot on the soil of Jinjira after crossing the river in a hired boat, they gazed at the shore they had left behind and felt as if Jinjira was an independent country, and that they had nothing more to fear. They observed that countless people were crossing the river and flooding this bank, and that as soon as they set foot on the soil on this bank, they felt soothed and reinvigorated. At that time, they didn't realize that, in fact, there was no place in the country to escape to; and after all, Jinjira was in close proximity. The illusory peace of mind under whose cloak Abdul Mojid and his family slept soundly for a night at his

Collegiate School classmate Anwar's house, in his village, Chorail, was shattered at dawn the next day by the Pakistani army when they fired artillery shells from across the river. When the operation at Jinjira concluded that afternoon, Abdul Mojid, his Ma and sisters realized that there was no place to escape to. When they sought to leave Anwar's house and flee in the face of the Pakistani army's attack and found that the army had formed a cordon, they took shelter in that two-storeyed house in a field where Abdul Mojid's physical apparatus broke down momentarily. After that, they returned the same evening to their house in Lakshmi Bazar, and they observed to their surprise and astonishment that, within two days, everyone else in the moholla had returned; only the houses of the Hindus remained uninhabited for the next nine months. The people of the moholla subsequently found out that after the 25th of March, every living being had left home, all except for two people. One of them was Khwaja Ahmed Ali, and on that Saturday evening, it was only he in all of Lakshmi Bazar who turned the lights on. The people of the moholla got to know that another person hadn't left home at this time, and that was Moulana Bodu. There was no need for him to leave, but the people of the moholla didn't see him even once until the end of the month of March. Later, they found out that he had been hiding in his own house. That was because after hearing the sound of gunfire and ammunition and witnessing the rising flames in the sky of

Dhaka, he realized that 'Joy Bangla' was finished; and in this interregnum between the end of crisis and the arrival of good times for him, he didn't want to suddenly die in any stray incident. The people of the moholla later learnt that he hid himself for those few days in the storeroom that lay in darkness beside the kitchen of his house. The people of the moholla were not able to recollect when Moulana Bodu emerged from there and was spotted in the street, but they say that the day they saw him walking along the street, wearing a long jobba, they were scared, and because of the fear, they felt a kind of hatred. They thought that it was as if they had never seen this person before and he hadn't seen them either, that he didn't know that on the night of the 25th of March, the houses and buildings of Lakshmi Bazar were submerged in the ghastly red glow of the fire blazing in Nayabazar, and that the sound of gunfire had left the people of the moholla utterly disoriented in terror. It occurred to them that, at a time when the people of the moholla were feeling imperilled, Moulana Bodu was the only person who was perfectly calm and composed in the midst of all that was happening. As he walked on the street after emerging from the storeroom, observing the terrified looks on the faces of his neighbours, he said, 'Assalamu Alaikum.' But still, even if the feelings they had regarding Moulana Bodu at this time were not so clear, the day the army first arrived in the moholla and discovered Moulana Bodu, the people at once realized that they had already recognized him for what he was. After that, it was as if the people of the moholla ventured through a ghastly contagion, from which they emerged only in the middle of December. The Pakistani army entered the narrow lane of the moholla on two occasions in 1971. The people of the moholla said that the first time the army arrived there, their principal objective was to find Moulana Bodu; he had stood out at once, saying, 'Hajir, hujur. Present, sir,' and after that the people came to know him as the enforcer of justice in the moholla. On that first day, the army left after shooting and killing seven people and Moulana Bodu's younger son's pet dog, Bhulu. Before the leader of the soldiers, Captain Imran, got into the jeep, he thought that he ought to piss, and so he stood under a lamp post at the edge of a wall with his legs spread, undid the buttons at the fly of his trousers, and pissed luxuriously. Meanwhile, the other soldiers boarded their truck, and the driver of the captain's jeep waited with the engine running; at that time, it was only Moulana Bodu who stood meekly under the noontime sun, with his palms placed one over the other below his navel, observing the captain pissing. While the people of the moholla were sitting silently beside the seven bodies and Moulana Bodu's younger son was weeping for his dead Bhulu, Moulana Bodu was standing behind the tall, young Pakistani captain and observing the liquid stream emerging from between his legs and spreading over the earth like the streaks of a bolt of lightning. The sound of the pissing occupied his entire auditory faculty, and the captain executed the act with such luxury that it seemed like he would continue to do the deed eternally, and that the dull sound of the captain pissing, which occupied Moulana Bodu's entire consciousness, would waft like a faint melody all his life. Those who had seen Moulana Bodu in the moholla at that time had said that it had seemed to them that Moulana Bodu was in a dreamlike state. When the captain was done pissing, he buttoned up and turned around, and Moulana Bodu's eyes then fell on the colourful bubbles of foam accumulated over the ground which the captain had assailed with his piss. The captain of the Pakistani army of occupation acknowledged Moulana Bodu once again, who was still standing in that way, and patted him on his back before getting into his jeep. Moulana Bodu had then smiled, and the people of the moholla were unable to convey to anyone now what that smile was like; they said that only those people who had seen the illumination of that smile on the face of Moulana Bodu at the captain's touch could understand it. Moulana Bodu was standing on the street in the moholla, dressed in a long jobba with a scarf slung over his shoulder and that smile on his face. The people of the moholla subsequently observed that Moulana Bodu no longer wore that grey-coloured jobba. They said that they had thought that the captain had actually wet his hand while buttoning the fly of his trousers, and that he had wiped his wet hand on the cloth on Moulana Bodu's back because he did not have a kerchief in his pocket. But they later came to know that Moulana Bodu had preserved the jobba to honour and keep alive the memory of the captain having touched him. After Moulana Bodu fled in the month of December, on the day people removed all the things in his house and deposited them in Ajij Pathan's house, his wife had looked at everything and said that it was all theirs except for a jobba and a scarf. The people of the moholla then spotted that grey-coloured jobba of Moulana Bodu's after a long time, and they remembered that the Pakistani captain had wiped his piss on this garment, and that Moulana Bodu's face had lit up in a celestial smile as a result. The people of the moholla then carried Moulana Bodu's jobba and scarf atop a pole to the end of the street and set them on fire. That was on the 31st of December in 1971. But two years later, when a general amnesty was declared and Moulana Bodu returned to Lakshmi Bazar, the people of the moholla once again saw him wearing that grey poplin jobba; only the smile on his face was absent. And now it was as if Moulana Bodu had begun once again from scratch, and once again the people of the moholla observed him walking with his eyes fixed to the ground. The day after he returned, he humbly exchanged greetings with everyone in the moholla and went to meet the families of the eight people killed in the moholla in 1971. The people of the moholla later spoke about their conviction that, through that foolhardy act, he had merely wanted to examine the scars of seven wounds. Then, that Tuesday afternoon, Abdul Mojid saw Moulana Bodu standing humbly beneath the kamini tree near the gate of their compound. 'How are you all?' The mockery concealed in this question was so cruel that, hearing it spoken inside the compound of his own house, and seeing Moulana Bodu there, Abdul Mojid was rendered speechless. His Ma then came out to the veranda and spotted Moulana Bodu. 'How are you all?' It was as if this courteous enquiry crossed the limits of Abdul Mojid's Ma's tolerance. The wrathful, furious and grieving woman quickly stepped down from the veranda to the compound and screamed, cursing him and lamenting loudly, *Thuk dei, thuk dei, thuk dei mukhe!* I spit on you, I spit on you, I spit on your face!' This woman had lamented the same way, one day, when she saw the lacerated dead body of her daughter. Moulana Bodu was not to be found then; he had fled. On that most melancholy evening in December 1971, when Abdul Mojid found his sister's dead body and carried it home, he had wrapped her in a sari. Abdul Mojid had seen Momena's body unclothed, as had his mother, and seeing her daughter's mutilated body, Abdul Mojid's Ma's grief had congealed. She had not let her daughter be given her final bath, and she compelled the people of the moholla to bury her wrapped in the sari, without a shroud. As if providing an illusory cloak of justification, from the margins of her senselessness she had declared to everyone in the

moholla that she would present her daughter's corpse in
this bloodied and shroudless state before Allah's throne, in
the field of Al-Hashr. She had fondled the face of the slain
Momena laid on the cot in the veranda, she had kissed the
lips encrusted with blood and dirt, and looking at
Momena's half shut eyes, she had lamented, *'Ma re, ma re,
ma re!* Oh my child, oh my precious, oh my precious child!'
Standing under the kamini tree, all the people of the
moholla had then cast their eyes down, all the women and
children of the moholla had whimpered and wept, and the
huge tree itself had veritably grieved. The people of the
moholla once again heard Abdul Mojid's Ma's lament on
a cold Tuesday afternoon, 'I spit on you, I spit on you, I
spit on your face!' The people of Lakshmi Bazar found out
why Abdul Mojid's Ma was lamenting again; a different
Moulana Bodu was now manifest in the moholla. On that
wintry Tuesday, the widows of the slain Khwaja Ahmed
Ali and Khwaja Shofiq, Alauddin's Ma, Abu Korim, who
had lost his son, and three more men and women, were all
dumbfounded on seeing Moulana Bodu standing in the
compounds of their houses. The people of the moholla
found out that, upon spotting Moulana Bodu, Khwaja
Ahmed Ali's widow, Khwaja Shofiq's Ma, had stepped
down quickly and stopped Moulana Bodu from coming any
further. Those who were then present in the moholla had
heard a warning cry emitted in a woman's voice, 'Beware,
beware!' Those who saw Jainab Begum then later reported

that, seeing her with the prayer beads hanging from her raised hand, it had seemed to them that she wanted to prevent the return of Azazel into her compound, and seeing the fire in her eyes, Moulana Bodu left the courtyard without saying a word, hastily removing himself as if he were an apparition. The people of the moholla had also heard about Alauddin's Ma and Abu Korim's wife. They found out that when Abu Korim's wife looked out from her window and spotted Moulana Bodu standing in the courtyard, she had collapsed in a faint on top of the metal utensils scattered over the kitchen floor. When there was a hue and cry in the household over the fainted woman, Moulana Bodu left the place. And they got to know that, not finding anyone in the outer compound of the departed Alauddin's house, as soon as Moulana Bodu went through the alleyway and reached the inner courtyard, he had fallen into danger. When Alauddin's Ma saw Moulana Bodu standing in front of her as she was about to enter the house after washing utensils beside the well, she lost all sense of propriety. The people of the moholla came to know that Alauddin's Ma had flung the utensils in her hand at Moulana Bodu's face. Later, a person from the adjacent house who had witnessed everything said that, while he was standing on the roof of his house, he had seen a person running through the alleyway of Alauddin's house like a chased fox, exiting through the gate of the courtyard and fleeing. He said that the person was Moulana Bodu, and

that he saw the slain Alauddin's Ma, a veritable Goddess
Durga at war, running behind him, brandishing the
blowpipe used to ignite the clay stove. He also said that,
while running out, Moulana Bodu stumbled against the
frame of the gate and fell to the ground, and then the
woman at his heels flung the iron blowpipe at him. Those
who were not present in the moholla that afternoon later
heard about it in detail until late into the night from those
who had witnessed the incident or heard about it from
someone else. The people of Lakshmi Bazar had spoken to
one another the next morning about not having been able
to sleep. They had said that their wives lay restlessly in bed
that night, like grieving women, and that they had been
overwhelmed by a powerful flood of agitation. That
morning, the people of the moholla had seen Moulana
Bodu walking towards them, they had heard him saying,
'Assalamu Alaikum.' But the people of the moholla did not
respond; they had thought that their sleep-deprived bodies
were unwilling to do so, their mouths and tongues were not
eager to respond to Moulana Bodu. They had noticed that
there was a swelling near his nose and that he walked with
a limp. Seeing him, at first they thought that he was
returning from the mosque after the Fajr prayers, but they
found out later that he was actually returning, that early in
the morning, from Ajij Pathan's house. They learnt that,
after being chased by Alauddin's Ma the previous evening,
he had run to Ajij Pathan's residence. But since Pathan was

not at home then, he went back again at the break of dawn. When Ajij Pathan stepped into the living room wearing a lungi and a sleeveless vest with a shawl wrapped around him, in the midst of brushing his teeth, Moulana Bodu was standing like a criminal; his hands, clutching one another, hung below his waist and his eyes were fixed on the ruptured patches on the cement floor of Ajij Pathan's room. The people of the moholla subsequently heard that Moulana Bodu had not uttered a single word in Ajij Pathan's presence, he just stood there silent, bent. Ajij Pathan was brushing his teeth and spitting out quantities of filthy, foamy paste mixed with blood and saliva from the window. As he sought to stop the saliva and foam accumulated in his mouth from falling to the floor, he stutteringly told Moulana Bodu to now turn good; he said that since his leader had pardoned others like Moulana Bodu, he had no vengefulness of his own. The people of the moholla got to know that when Moulana Bodu heard him say that, tears had streamed down from his eyes and fallen to the floor, and looking at him, Ajij Pathan had said in discomfiture, '*Kainden na, kainden na.* Don't cry, don't cry.' The people of the moholla also found out something else, which was that on the Tuesday night which they had spent sleeplessly, it was only Ajij Pathan who slept. Because he was not at home on that Tuesday afternoon, he had not heard the lamentation of the seven men and women of the moholla. Returning home tired, late at night, he fell asleep. Seeing Moulana Bodu early in the morning, he was perturbed; observing his silent, doleful face, he was unable to say anything. He remembered that when he had returned to the moholla after the victory, he had heard about the seven people in the moholla who were killed, he had seen the sorrowful faces of the widows and the men and women who had lost their sons, he had visited the twin graves in the courtyard of Khwaja Ahmed Ali, and he had witnessed the festive burning of Moulana Bodu's jobba at the mouth of the moholla's street. Ajij Pathan also remembered the appearance of his own ransacked house that day. But with his gums injured by the toothbrush, looking at Moulana Bodu, he thought that Moulana Bodu had been exactly the same before the 25th of March in 1971, gloomy and bowed, and the people of the moholla found out that the day after the Tuesday evening when Momena's Ma's lamentations were heard – 'I spit on your face' – Ajij Pathan had said to the tearful Moulana Bodu, 'Don't cry, Moulana, don't cry.' But after that, when Moulana Bodu encountered everyone and walked on saying, 'Slamalekum,' the people of the moholla were indifferent, because Momena's Ma's screams from the previous day were still alive in their sleep-deprived consciousnesses; but Moulana Bodu was no longer perturbed by such behaviour on the part of the people of the moholla. When the story of Moulana Bodu shedding tears at Ajij Pathan's house spread in the moholla, the people of the moholla got to hear his own view on the matter. They found out that Moulana Bodu had said that only a respectable person knew how to accord dignity to another respectable person. Quoting from the children's storybooks from school, he declared that, like the brave King Porus, he had gone and stood in front of Alexander the victor, and he had seen that Alexanders always conducted themselves with Poruses in the same way; because only someone brave could recognize the features of a brave man. The people of the moholla couldn't comprehend all this talk from Moulana Bodu. Many of them didn't know about King Porus or Alexander, they couldn't figure out where Moulana Bodu's bravery lay. They forgot about it all. But after a long time, Abdul Mojid reflected once again on the significance of the conduct of Alexander and King Porus and found himself in a crisis. On the day following that day after the strike, when all the parties had addressed the people as 'brothers' and thanked them and the strap on Abdul Mojid's sandal went *phot* and snapped, he encountered Ajij Pathan briefly on the street; in the course of talking about a few things, Abdul Mojid also remarked that Moulana Bodu now addressed them as 'brothers' and thanked them for the strike. When Ajij Pathan heard that, it was as if he had glimpsed into the core of Abdul Mojid's heart, and smiling despondently, he placed his veined arm which resembled the branch of an ancient tree on his shoulder. He took him to his house after a long time, and said so many things to him, almost none of which Abdul Mojid could understand, all except for one thing, which was that, after all, in politics there was no such thing as friends for life or enemies for life, and so, what else could people do but forget the past? But the people of Lakshmi Bazar who kept on forgetting the past saw that their past broke unremittingly through the soil and sprang up, like shoots of grass. They now forgot the fact that even the right to assemble at the mosque was not forever; because when they saw the red flames of Nayabazar hanging like a curtain from the sky on the morning of the 25th of March in 1971, like terrified creatures, they had thought they ought to escape; but on that Friday, no muezzin's voice echoed from the mosque, that day no one offered the Friday prayers while the curfew was on. The situation had then reached such a pass that the name of Allah was constantly on their lips, and they had escaped the moholla, whispering, 'Allah, Allah.' After that, everyone had returned to the moholla once again, like chased rats. There was no discussion among them regarding where they wanted to flee to; they only knew the truth that there was no way of escaping and no place to escape to in the country. That was when they had seen Moulana Bodu come walking towards them; he had told them that they had nothing to fear, that Allah would protect Muslims, and after that he began to set crows flying in the moholla. Following that, the day the Pakistani army first arrived at the moholla,

Moulana Bodu salaamed and stood there, and they shot seven people dead. After the captain of the Pakistani army pissed luxuriously and left with his soldiers, then, standing there, Moulana Bodu let that sweet smile of his spread across his face, and he turned around and looked at the houses and buildings of the moholla. It occurred to the people of the moholla who had seen him then, that owing to some inexplicable wind-induced phenomenon, Moulana Bodu's frame expanded, and on that darkest day of the moholla, he stood suspended like a scarecrow, gazing at the sky. But when he found out that the people of the moholla said they had heard the azan called out by Khwaja Ahmed Ali, and that he had concluded the azan, he screamed and raised a hue and cry that echoed through the dark, curfewed night. Moulana Bodu told the moholla folk that they should have known that Khwaja Ahmed Ali was a munafiq, a hypocrite. But when the people of the moholla failed to remember anything to that effect, Moulana Bodu became furious. In the morning, while burying Khwaja Ahmed Ali and his son with due obsequies in the courtyard of their house, when the people of the moholla said that Khwaja Ahmed Ali had concluded the azan and that at the end of the azan he had pronounced four times that 'only Allah is great', Moulana Bodu swore at them, saying they were idol-worshipping kafirs, and added that Khwaja Ahmed Ali was no angel, and that he had certainly not concluded calling out the azan. Because when Khwaja Ahmed Ali was shot

on the roof, Moulana Bodu had been at the top of the flight
of stairs and had heard the azan being terminated as soon
as the sound of the gunshot was heard. But the people of
the moholla did not buy that; they contended that only the
azan called out in the heavenly voice of Belal could have
sounded as sweet. Hearing that, Moulana Bodu went away,
and when he returned once again, the people had just
finished pressing the earth down over the graves and they
stood up. They saw that Moulana Bodu's servants were
bringing the dead body of Bhulu, fussing noisily. They
recalled that, on that day, they had seen something even
more terrifying than a snake in Moulana Bodu's eyes, and
observing him, they had turned silent and frozen. Moulana
Bodu's men noisily dug the earth and buried the dog in the
courtyard of Khwaja Ahmed Ali's house, beside the two
graves there, and then casting his eyes towards the terrified
folk, he said, *'Ei kobore kono pir nai, kutta achhe.* There's no
pir in this grave, only a dog.' Gazing at his face then, the
people of the moholla had thought that they would have to
wait before responding to Moulana Bodu. But the way
events unfolded, they saw that, in fact, they never got to say
anything to Moulana Bodu; rather, it was he who, once
again, did the talking. The day the people of the moholla
buried Khwaja Ahmed Ali, they had been able to grasp that
Moulana Bodu wanted to throw a detestable dog's corpse
over their feelings of reverence for him. But in 1980, the

people of the moholla discovered that the dead body of this dog was dearer to Moulana Bodu than the seven human corpses. Standing before the gathering in Victoria Park that day, Moulana Bodu said that, apart from his son's death, he had witnessed two unfortunate deaths in 1971; in fact, he had witnessed only one death, and that was the death of his beloved son's dog, Bhulu. He had felt sad when Bhulu died. He had not seen the other death take place; he had heard about it later. That was the death of the razakar Abdul Goni. Pointing to the bench in question, Moulana Bodu showed the listeners the spot and proclaimed that those who happened to be sitting on that bench then didn't know that Abdul Goni had been martyred there, and hearing him say that, the people of Lakshmi Bazar and Kolta Bazar, Patuatuli and Armanitola who were listening to him had thought that perhaps he was referring to some other Abdul Goni. But despite thinking so, they realized that he was referring to the selfsame Abdul Goni who had identified twenty-one missing people as being dead as he sucked Vita Cola through a straw, and after which the people of all these mohollas had gone in a grieving procession and dug up and recovered fifty-six skulls from beside the Christian cemetery. Gazing at the skulls arrayed over banana leaves, the enraged public had then suddenly remembered Abdul Goni. Their grieving rage had blazed, and they then left the Christian cemetery and ran towards Victoria Park from every direction. When they reached Victoria Park, they saw that Abdul Goni's severed head lay in the dirt. It was never found out who killed Abdul Goni, but they figured out that any relative of those twenty-one people whom Abdul Goni had identified as dead could have committed the murder; anyone from the old Nayabazar neighbourhoods that were reduced to ashes, or else anyone from among the residents of Lakshmi Bazar, Kolta Bazar, Patuatuli, English Road or Narinda who had stared death in the face for nine months, could have committed the murder. The public was not shocked that Abdul Goni was killed. They untied the rope and lowered his body from the bench to a mat, and gathered together the bloodied Vita Cola bottle and the severed head, and uprooted all the grass together with the soil over which the tiniest drop of dark red blood had coagulated. After that, the public fetched a can of bleaching powder, and sprinkled it on the bench with Abdul Goni's blood and over the soil, and cleansed everything. The people of Lakshmi Bazar then remembered Moulana Bodu's younger son's dead dog. They ran towards Khwaja Ahmed Ali's and Khwaja Shofiq's graves; they carefully determined the exact location of the buried dog, and very slowly and with great care, removed the earth from above the buried remains of the dog that belonged to Moulana Bodu's family. They removed its bones from the earth so gently that Khwaja Ahmed Ali and Khwaja Shofiq, who were in eternal sleep in the earth, and the very earth itself, would have had no clue about what they were doing. The people of Lakshmi Bazar put the dog's bones in a jute sack and took it to Victoria Park. There, they gathered together Bhulu's remains and Abdul Goni's severed head and body and the bloodied soil, and taking everything to the middle of the Buriganga river, they threw it all into the water. After that, they forgot about those two creatures. Nine years after this, hearing about Abdul Goni from Moulana Bodu, they remembered everything once again; they recalled the smell of the bleaching powder. They pictured the five-foot-one-inch and one-hundred-pound Abdul Goni marching in the street of the moholla together with five other razakars. Seeing the six scarecrows marching down the street, calling out, 'Left-right,' the people of the moholla had been amused despite their fears. They had thought that they were surely watching some circus act; with their pants held up with strings, their loose canvas shoes and crumpled caps, the razakars looked like clowns. Then, after the 25th of March, amidst the desolation that had descended upon the moholla, four pairs of doves arrived and made their nests there. When people hid themselves inside their houses in the afternoons, the doves used to sit on the parapet and coo, and the people could hear the razakars marching down their street, saying, *'Lept, lept.'* Seeing them then, the womenfolk of the moholla couldn't help but giggle like young girls although they were plunged in distress and fear. They thought a row of ants was marching by. *'Kemun lal piprar lahan lage ekektare.* See, how each one looks like a red ant,' they had said. The people of the moholla did not know whether or not the razakars had heard their womenfolk and children joking about them, but it seemed that it was with this joke that the razakars began their activities there. Three days after they were first spotted in the moholla, they were weary after their parade and knocked on Abbas Ali's door to quench their thirst, and after that, when there was a delay in responding to the knock, they kicked the door thrice. Then, when the door was opened and the six-foot-tall Abbas Ali emerged, they asked him his name. The people of the moholla heard later that when Abbas Ali said his name, the six razakars had made a face to mock him and told him that his name was not Abbas Ali but Gaabgachh Ali, referring to the tall persimmon tree. After that, when they enquired about the reason for the delay in opening the door and he stuttered, one of the razakars hit the lanky Abbas Ali on his ribs with a lathi and said, *'Tui byata Gaabgachh Ali, tawre pitaya laash banamu.* Hey you, Gaabgaach Ali, we'll thrash you to death.' However, when the people of the moholla saw the dark bruise on Abbas Ali's ribs, they realized that this was no joke at all. After that, the clownlike razakars set up a slaughterhouse in the premises of the primary school, and the people of the moholla got a detailed account of the activities of this slaughterhouse at Victoria Park, after the barrel of a gun had been shoved up Abdul Goni's arse. Nine years after that, Moulana Bodu told them that Abdul Goni had been killed like a dog because of public rage – he said he had actually been martyred. Although the people of the moholla were not perturbed by that, nonetheless, they could see that truth changed with the passage of time. The people of the moholla felt that either nature or fate had perhaps chosen Abdul Goni for some reason from among the six razakars. He was the only one of the six who was caught after the war, and it was because of him that, one rainy day, the people of the moholla had turned rebellious despite all their fears, and after that the army had arrived at the moholla for the second time. Towards the end of the month of Shrabon, when it suddenly began raining in the moholla, Abdul Goni had hurriedly taken shelter at the gate of the deserted house of Mayarani's family. He had thought the rain would stop soon, but when it continued raining heavily for a long time, he became annoyed and weary with the load of the .303 rifle on his shoulder. He didn't put the rifle down, but he saw that a tulsi plant near the open gate was swaying under the beating rain. Mainly to overcome his annoyance, Abdul Goni first plucked a couple of leaves of the tulsi plant and chewed them, and after that he broke a branch of the plant. The people of the moholla learnt about this story later. They found out that the rainy-day incident commenced after he broke the branch of Mayarani's family's tulsi plant. The people of the moholla still saw Mayarani nowadays; she was a teacher in a primary school in Bonogram and was still unmarried. The people of the moholla were of the view that Mayarani had devoted her life to waiting for Mohammad Selim. But Abdul Mojid had a feeling that Mayarani was not waiting for Mohammad Selim, although Abdul Mojid couldn't figure out why she didn't get married. In 1972, when Mayarani's family returned to the moholla along with other Hindu folk but Mohammad Selim did not, and a note from Mayarani was found in his trunk, Abdul Mojid remembered the twenty-one letters hidden in the niche in their wall. He had removed the stone jammed in the mouth of the niche, taken out the dusty papers, and thus been transported once again to the perilousness of the past, when he was unable to make Mayarani accept them and wasn't able to return them to Mohammad Selim either. Seeing the letters of the missing Mohammad Selim once again, Abdul Mojid had felt guilty, and he had thought, at first, that he would hand the letters over to Mohammad Selim's Ma and reveal to her the secret behind the mysterious note from Mayarani. But he was unable to do that. He realized that this lie had now become more credible than the truth, and as a result of Mohammad Selim's death, it had already become devoid of meaning; it was pointless to raise the issue anew. And so, the twenty-one futile letters remained captive in the niche in the wall of Abdul Mojid's room for more than a decade. After that, one Sunday morning, six months after the day the strap of his sponge sandal snapped on the way to Raysha Bazar upon hearing Moulana Khayer speak, when Yasmin delivered a daughter, Abdul Mojid named her Momena, and that evening, when the unmarried Mayarani, looking pale like the fading afternoon light, came to see Abdul Mojid's newborn girl, he remembered Mohammad Selim once again. He looked at Mayarani's sad, dark-skinned face, but he was still unable to fathom her. When Mayarani left Yasmin's bedside after that and came to the sitting room, Abdul Mojid thought he could give it another try. He asked Mayarani to sit down. Then, standing on a chair, he removed the delicate pieces of paper from the ancient niche and said, *'Eguli loya jaan.* Take these with you.' Abdul Mojid held out the twenty-one letters towards Mayarani and she stared at him silently for a brief moment, but then, when she took the letters in the cup of her hands he was stunned. When Mayarani knotted Mohammad Selim's twenty-one letters into a fold at one end of the anchal of her sari like a bunch of withered shefali flowers and left without saying a word, at first Abdul Mojid thought that he was finally free of the debt of the laddus and biscuits he had consumed. After that, his heart went out to Mohammad Selim too; he thought that Mohammad Selim was eventually successful in everything: he went to war and liberated the country, and after long disregard, Mayarani accepted his love. But only a day later, Abdul Mojid's notion about the rehabilitation of Mohammad Selim's love was cast into doubt. His inner confusion became evident when, in the afternoon of the following day, Mayarani called him out, made him sit down in the courtyard and did a few things in front of him. Leaving Abdul Mojid sitting in the courtyard, she used a rusted knife to cut from its roots the large tulsi plant growing from the pedestal near the gate, and then took it afar and threw it away; after that, she dug up the earth on the pedestal and removed the base of roots too, and did away with them. Abdul Mojid remembered that, on a rainy day in the month of Shrabon in 1971, a rebellion had broken out in the moholla over the cutting of tulsi plants. In order to shelter from the pouring rain, the razakar Abdul Goni had stood under the gateway of Mayarani's house; he had broken off a branch from the tulsi plant and was chewing the leaves. After that, when the rain subsided and he went to Moulana Bodu's house with the tulsi branch in his hand and encountered him in the veranda, Moulana Bodu's brow became furrowed, '*Ki khao!* What are you chewing!' Moulana Bodu did not intend to ask him a question; he was rebuking him, because he was not unfamiliar with the tulsi leaf. But without realizing anything, Abdul Goni replied, '*Tulsipata khai.* I'm chewing tulsi leaves.' Moulana Bodu was furious when he heard that, nonetheless he controlled himself and asked, '*Tulsipata khao ken?* Why are you eating tulsi leaves?' The dim-witted Abdul Goni didn't understand even then, and he again thought this was another question, and he said, '*Tulsir pata chibote bhalo lage.*

I like to chew tulsi leaves.' Moulana Bodu then roared out, *'Nadaan,'* meaning nincompoop, and snatched the tulsi branch and flung it into the courtyard. He snarled, *'Tulsi gachh Hindura puja kore, ei gachh Hindu gachh.* Hindus worship the tulsi plant, this is a Hindu plant.' Moulana Bodu then remembered that the locality of Lakshmi Bazar was full of these plants, and he knew that every house in the moholla had one. He reckoned that the tulsi was useless as a plant and harmful to the soul. Within half an hour, he assembled six razakars in his compound and imparted to them his thoughts about tulsi plants; after that, he instructed them to cut down all the tulsi plants immediately. As a result of this instruction, once again, like when the Pakistani army had first arrived in the moholla, the razakars began stalking the compound, well-side and alleyway of every house. They pulled out or cut from the base all the tulsi plants from every house, whether Hindu or Muslim, and threw them at a spot on the road. While tearing out the tulsi plants in this way, the matter became complicated when, right at the end, a razakar entered Abdul Mojid's compound, uprooted one large and two small tulsi plants from near the well in the rear courtyard, and noticed while bringing those out that a joba, or hibiscus, red like blood, was in full bloom. It then occurred to the razakar that Hindus used joba flowers in their worship, and that, like the tulsi, the joba was also a Hindu plant and worthless. He then tried to break the tall and clustering joba plant from its base, and when he was unable to do that, he started breaking the branches. Abdul Mojid's sister, Momena, saw him doing that and she lost her self-control. The people of the moholla later came to know that when Momena tried to stop him from destroying the hibiscus plant, the razakar did not pay her any heed, and then the girl brought a chopper from the kitchen and drove the trespasser out. The people of the moholla found out about everything soon after, because they too got involved in the matter. Although the razakar who was chased away had been afraid because he was unarmed, his courage returned as soon as he joined the others, and his wounded masculinity awakened. He incited his associates to cut all the flowering plants, and the people of the moholla saw the razakars preparing to enter the compounds of their houses again. They objected to that, and as a result, first they had an altercation with the razakars, and after that, once all the people got together and the razakars tried to force their way in again, a scuffle ensued and a person landed a mighty slap on the face of an isolated razakar. It happened all of a sudden, and the razakar who was slapped wasn't even able to figure out who had slapped him, because he had been looking in another direction then. The people of the moholla, for their part, refused to identify the person; they said they had not seen anyone slapping him. But within a moment, the people of the moholla realized the terrible outcome the incident would have. They returned hastily to their respective homes with a great sense of dread. At first, the six razakars stood flabbergasted on the street; after that, it seemed the razakar who was slapped was the first one to return to his senses. Casting his eyes on the empty street and the closed gates of the houses, he roared out, *'Mandar polara!* You sons of swine!' The group then ran towards all the closed doorways and began kicking them hard, and in this state of frenzy, the razakar who was slapped brandished his .303 rifle and fired crazily into the air; the shot hit the parapet of a house, breaking the plaster, and then ricocheted and perforated the door. The people of the moholla got to know later that when Moulana Bodu heard the gunshot, he was initially scared; after that, when he was informed that his razakars were furious, he came out and saw everything, and once they had calmed down a bit, he heard about all that had happened. When Moulana Bodu heard that a razakar had been slapped, he became very concerned. When there was no more sound of gunfire, a couple of people from the moholla who were brave enough to peep out saw the razakars marching behind Moulana Bodu. That day, after a little while, the Pakistani army arrived at the moholla for the second time, and the people of the moholla witnessed the unfolding of an incident they would never forget. It was later found out that when Moulana Bodu heard about everything from the razakars, he had become agitated because he could sense that underlying it all was the resurrection of courage in the moholla folk after it had been broken and crushed. He concluded that the people of the moholla needed to be shown military might once again. Soon after receiving the intelligence from him, a military truck thudded into the narrow street of the moholla and halted near the heap of discarded tulsi plants. What the people of the moholla then felt was what any creature would feel in such a situation, which was the urge to flee. But the people of Lakshmi Bazar remembered what they had realized in the past, that there was no place to escape to anywhere in the country, so now, suppressing their fierce desire to flee, they remained in their respective homes. It was later learnt that on receiving word of the arrival of the Pakistani army, Moulana Bodu welcomed the leader of this squad, a lieutenant from Makran, and took him home. Moulana Bodu then informed him about the uprising that had taken place in the moholla. After enquiring about and ascertaining the facts regarding all aspects of the incident, the dark-skinned, youthful lieutenant asked, 'Kya aap aurat ko sambhaal nahi sakte? Can't you deal with a woman?' Moulana Bodu felt extremely embarrassed hearing this, and he said that although the uprising had been initiated by a woman, eventually all the menfolk of the moholla participated in it, and it was only one man who'd had the audacity to slap a razakar engaged in protecting law and order. The lieutenant from Makran was of the same view as Moulana Bodu regarding conducting an operation in the moholla, but he was unable to overcome his curiosity and he proposed, 'Let's see the heroine first.' Moulana Bodu could figure out who the 'heroine' referred to was, but he couldn't understand the full meaning of this sentence in English; the lieutenant then explained what he wanted in Urdu, and Moulana Bodu dispatched two razakars to fetch Momena. But the razakars could not find Momena at home, and none of the people in the moholla had seen her leaving her house; her Ma told the razakars that she had left just a little while ago to visit her aunt in Cumilla. The razakars were dumbstruck out of sheer anger and astonishment when they heard Abdul Mojid's Ma say that. They had no doubt at all that the woman was lying, but even after searching and ransacking the house, they couldn't find Momena. Those who were peeping through their windows or the gaps between their doors at this time then saw the unforgettable incident being enacted on the street. They saw some soldiers jumping out of the truck into the street; they had Chinese automatic rifles in their hands. At first, they walked up and down the street for a bit, and after that two of them went and stood facing the wall and pissed. At the same time, one soldier picked up a tulsi branch and began plucking out the leaves and throwing them on the ground. The people of the moholla understood that he had started doing that simply in order to while away the time. But by doing that, he came under the spell of the tulsi. While tearing off the leaves, he first got a whiff of its exceptional fragrance, and so he bit off a small piece of a green-purple leaf, and then put the entire leaf into his mouth. After the monotonous routine of eating roti and kabab in the cantonment, his war-weary tongue instantly awakened with the jolt of the sharp aromatic flavour. The razakars returned just then after completing their mission, and without looking at the soldiers who were chewing tulsi leaves, they went inside Moulana Bodu's house and reported their failure. The failure of the razakars strengthened the resolve of the young lieutenant to direct an operation in the moholla. When he came and stood outside with Moulana Bodu, he saw that his soldiers were standing around a heap of shrubs, rifles on their shoulders and tulsi branches in their hands; all of them were chewing the leaves. The lieutenant and Moulana Bodu discovered that the men had eaten almost all the tulsi leaves, and all that remained was a heap of leafless skeletons of shrubs. Beholding this sight, Moulana Bodu was stunned. And the lieutenant became perturbed. When Moulana Bodu asked them what they were doing, they replied, *Yeh ilaaj hai*. It's medicinal.' He despondently turned towards the lieutenant and said that their souls had been sullied. But when the lieutenant heard that, he thought that, having consumed half a maund of the muddy leaves, they would surely suffer food poisoning very soon. He couldn't help thinking that this too was perhaps a trap laid by the freedom fighters. Under these circumstances, the military operation in the moholla was suspended and the lieutenant hurriedly left the moholla with the soldiers to get them medical attention. Fifteen years after this, on a desolate afternoon, when Mayarani sat Abdul Mojid down in front of her and dug up by its roots the tulsi plant that had grown in the soil on the pedestal near the gate, he was astounded. He was unable to ask her anything. Because he had never really conversed much with Mayarani; besides, he thought that Mayarani would not speak to him right now in the midst of all these mysterious acts. He saw that after cutting the plant and pulling it out by its roots, Mayarani placed in the courtyard a tender sapling of tulsi, a bell-metal pot with water, a small bundle wrapped in pink cloth, and an oil lamp. After that, when Mayarani sat on her haunches and unwrapped the bundle, Abdul Mojid spotted the twenty-one letters. It seemed to him that Mayarani was performing some astonishing ritual; she struck a match and lit the wick of the lamp, then she burnt to ashes the twenty-one letters from Mohammad Selim, one by one, and put those ashes on the soil in the pedestal. Although Abdul Mojid was saddened by what he witnessed, he waited, and then he saw that after mixing the ashes from the burnt papers with the soil in the pedestal, Mayarani took the tender tulsi sapling and planted it in the earth with great care. After that, she pushed a stick in next to its base for support and poured water on the plant from the pot. At this stage, Abdul Mojid's sense of surprise and sadness turned into a kind of puzzlement, and he thought that his puzzlement would

never be resolved, because Mayarani would never explain
her actions. Mayarani had only answered the other question
of his, which had been in his mind but he had not actually
uttered, because he thought that her objective in bringing
him there and doing all this was so that he knew that the
letters no longer existed. Returning home after witnessing
Mayarani's performance, the confusion in Abdul Mojid's
mind regarding the matter of the success or failure of the
long-dead and forgotten Mohmmad Selim's love persisted.
When his Ma then placed his newborn daughter, wrapped
in a kantha, in his arms, he saw that his daughter's tiny face
was like a brown-coloured cloth; he thought that his
daughter would be dark-skinned as well, like his Ma and
Momena. Remembering Momena vividly again, as the
newborn daughter's grandmothers, mother and aunt soon
began discussing the matter of the name to be given her,
Abdul Mojid hugged his daughter who was cradled in his
arms to his chest and said, 'Let's name this girl Momena.'
Everyone was stunned. His aged Ma became immersed in
digging into the joys and agonies of the memories
concerning her own firstborn's arrival and the incident
surrounding her death, and the others realized that this
name was connected to the emotions and very existence of
the people of this family. Abdul Mojid's daughter was
named Momena. With the return of Big Momena in Little
Momena, Abdul Mojid had no doubt that they had failed
to save Big Momena. Following the skirmish in the

moholla over the hibiscus plant, when the razakars arrived at Abdul Mojid's house in search of Momena, she was lying prostrate on the floor of a deserted and broken-down hut by the well-side; her body was completely buried under ash and clay, and only three tubes of papaya-leaf stems connected her nostrils and mouth to the air outside; and over this mound sat a hen brooding over seven eggs. The razakars arrived and searched the whole house, but they couldn't find Momena; her Ma told them that she had gone to visit her aunt. That day, Momena lay buried under mud and ash. She later said that she had been sleeping then and woke up only when, late at night, Abdul Mojid removed the earth over her using a spade. Emerging from this grave, Momena took shelter under the cot in their middle room. The people of the moholla did not see Momena again, they had heard that she had gone to Cumilla; but on the 10th of December, when airplanes were dropping bombs over Dhaka and the nation was waiting to be liberated at any moment, they came to know only when the razakars took her away that Momena had been in her house all along. The people of the neighbourhood found out that Momena had been hiding under the cot and only came out at night. Nevertheless, the razakars got word of it, and on the 10th of December, they arrived during curfew time and entered Abdul Mojid's compound. When Abdul Mojid's Ma told them that her daughter was in Cumilla, they laughed and entered the house and dragged Momena out from under the cot. At that time, when Abdul Mojid arrived on the scene and held his sister's arm, a razakar pressed the barrel of his rifle to his stomach, and Momena said, '*Dorais na, amare kichhu korbo na.* Don't be afraid, nothing will happen to me.' After saying that, late in the afternoon on the 10th of December in 1971, Momena released her arm from Abdul Mojid's grip and left with the razakars; she never returned. Abdul Mojid and his Ma had then run to Moulana Bodu's house, and his Ma had fallen at Moulana Bodu's feet, in the way people lay in prostration to Allah. Abdul Mojid had observed that the foam of saliva from his half-senseless Ma dampened Moulana Bodu's pump shoes. When Moulana Bodu heard Abdul Mojid's Ma's plea, as razakars patrolled behind sandbags on the roof and near the gate of the house, he made a joke even in this dire situation, '*Apner maiya na Cumilla thake!* Isn't your daughter supposed to be in Cumilla!' And he then freed his legs and went inside the house. After that, they didn't see Moulana Bodu again in the moholla for two years. Abdul Mojid found Momena four days later at the western end of Rayer Bazar, beside the Buriganga river, on ground that looked like a sandbank. Abdul Mojid could not figure out whether she had been alive those four days. Now, he often remembered the moment he found Momena after having searched frantically for her. After walking through the deserted Kumar Para locality of Rayer Bazar, when he reached and stood atop elevated ground, he had seen a few dry sandbank-like fields and some marshy patches lying next to one another, and far in the distance, the water of the narrow strip of river shimmering in the light of the sun. He had spotted Momena lying on one of the sandbank-like fields. He covered that bit of distance and reached there, or one could say, and he now claimed, that God carried him across that bit of distance and placed him beside his dead sister. He then looked at her. One of her breasts had been cut off, there were severe lacerations from her stomach down to her thighs, and her whole right thigh lay sliced open like a watermelon; she was lying on her back, her body pressing down upon her hands that were tied behind her, and her face was raised to the sky. He fell to his knees, his heart wailed out, and as if in a state of delirium, he merely uttered, 'Allah, Allah.' Bending down over Momena's face and gazing at her half-open eyes staring at the sky, he wept, crying, 'Aapa, Aapa.' Later, when Abdul Mojid named his daughter Momena, he didn't do that because he was forgetting her name; rather, he did that because this was a name that ought not to be forgotten. Abdul Mojid didn't come to know about the reaction of the people of the moholla to his naming his daughter Momena, or whether there was any reaction at all, or whether they even knew about the matter. But, one day, Abdul Mojid realized to his great astonishment that it was Moulana Bodu who

retained the memories of 1971 the most. Moulana Bodu
had not forgotten that the razakars had taken Momena
away and killed her, and for that matter, after the country
had been liberated, when he returned to the moholla and
was chased by Alauddin's mother, he realized that the
people of this community too had not forgotten anything.
Because Moulana Bodu, who hardly ever spoke to Abdul
Mojid unless it was absolutely necessary, stopped him one
day on the road, and enquired about the well-being of his
baby daughter, and after that he said, *'Boiner naame naam
rakhchho, boinere bhulo naika?* You named her after your
sister, you haven't forgotten her, have you?' Abdul Mojid
knew for certain that he would never forget Momena. But
hearing Moulana Bodu, what occurred to him was that
Moulana Bodu knew that Abdul Mojid's family had not
forgotten about the nine months of 1971. Abdul Mojid
became worried. He remembered the day his sandal had
snapped on the way to Raysha Bazar, and when he had
heard Moulana Bodu's son thanking the public, he had felt
as if he had been flogged, and that day, Ajij Pathan had
taken him to his house, and placing his arm over his
shoulder, had told him that people needed to forget a lot
of things as time went by, because reality often loomed
large. However, Abdul Mojid could now see that no one
ever forgets anything, and that Moulana Bodu too knew
that. In such a situation, after thinking over the matter for
a few days, he decided to leave the moholla. Of course, he

took the opinions of his Ma, his wife and also the husbands of his two sisters on the matter, but his decision to sell the house in Lakshmi Bazar and set up home anew in Badda, near his in-laws' house, remained unchanged. After thinking over a few things, he thought that this was the only logical decision. First of all, he didn't want his daughter to fall victim, like his sister, to the bloodlust of Moulana Bodu or his sons, and he thought that if reality proceeded in this way, one could never be certain that this wouldn't happen. He knew that Moulana Bodu was practising the same politics now as he had in 1971, and that he was aware that Abdul Mojid and his family continued to hate him for Momena's death. He felt that in this changed political situation, if Moulana Bodu and his party ever got the chance, they wouldn't spare him for that hatred. But Abdul Mojid also realized that if Moulana Bodu did get that chance, almost everyone in the moholla would see his old visage again; but it wouldn't be practical to think that all the residents of the moholla would sell off their houses and escape on account of such a fear. Nonetheless, Abdul Mojid decided that there was nothing to be gained by thinking about what would befall all the people of the moholla; he wanted to save himself first, and he could do that even in the absence of any collective endeavour – by leaving the moholla right away. As a result of such thinking and his final decision, an advertisement regarding the sale of Abdul Mojid's house was published in *The Daily Ittefaq* on the 7th of January 1986. And it can be assumed that if their house was sold, their names were obliterated from the neighbourhood of Lakshmi Bazar. The people of the moholla might have initially been surprised at this conduct on their part; but after a time they could perhaps fathom why Abdul Mojid had left the moholla and gone away, or it could also be said that perhaps no one at all in the moholla and in the country understood the nature of Abdul Mojid's crisis any more.

Abu Ibrahim's Death

Man dies for sure
but the significance of each death is different.
Sima Qian,
a litterateur in ancient China
had said,
'A man dies only once. The death maybe as weighty
as Mount Tai
or it may be lighter than a goose feather.'

WHEN THE CORPSE BEARERS WHO were gathered under the guava tree in the compound of her house on Kalibari Road in Sirajganj lifted the bier with Abu Ibrahim's dead body to their shoulders and left the compound to walk towards Jame Masjid, his plump widow, Mamata, amidst her grief and that cruel reality, remembered a long-ago night. Abu Ibrahim had woken her up in the middle of the night, taken her to the balcony of their flat in the government housing estate on Bailey Road in Dhaka, and whispered to her,

'A herd of sarus cranes is flying by, listen.' As the corpse bearers and those following behind advanced along Kalibari Road reciting the Kalema Tayyaba loudly, Mamata recalled that night for some reason, and her heart was torn, her eyes awash like the Jamuna during the rains. And that night, the night the sarus cranes had flown over Bailey Road, robbed of the snug comfort of sleep, Mamata had got angry and uttered a sentence, a sentence which we'll hear her utter many times hereafter, and as a result we may perhaps think that Abu Ibrahim was essentially what Mamata had called him. That night, before pushing Abu Ibrahim away and going back to sleep, Mamata had said to him, 'You're mad.' Actually, is a man ever mad, or can a man ever avoid being mad? After Mamata went back to sleep, Abu Ibrahim stood in the veranda of his quarters and listened until late into the night to the sound of the faraway birds flying over slumbering Dhaka. And the next day, Mamata and Bindu created such a scene that Abu Ibrahim had to get involved in the matter, and this time Mamata didn't let him off by merely calling him mad.

When we observe Abu Ibrahim and Mamata together, we often think of all those protagonists of Greek tragedies who accept their fate and carry the burden all their lives. A sign of restlessness was noticeable in the pupils of Abu Ibrahim's eyes and in the exceptionally radiant smile on his gaunt face, a restlessness that he kept chained with abstinence. That's why he had no dissatisfaction regarding

Mamata, and Mamata too was content with her lot, of husband, children, family, and household. Such was the conjugal life of the thin, wordy and rustic Abu Ibrahim, and the plump, fair-skinned, small-town Mamata, and in the evening of the day after the sarus cranes flew over the housing estate on Bailey Road, Mamata didn't let him off by merely calling him mad, she swore at him, calling him a chamar, a low-born; that afternoon, Abu Ibrahim had taken a nap, and when he woke up, he saw that Mamata was scolding their daughter Bindu. He listened for a while and then rose and went into the bathroom. Emerging after washing his face, he saw Bindu standing beside the small concrete slab that had been placed for cooking purposes inside all the flats in this housing estate, her face buried in her palms atop the slab. She was sobbing quietly. Abu Ibrahim wiped his face with a towel, then Mamata suddenly noticed that there was Bindu sobbing right in front of him, and all Abu Ibrahim could do was rub his jaw with the towel, so it was natural for her to get agitated at that.

'Hey girl, stop crying!'

'What happened?'

Mamata didn't respond to Abu Ibrahim's query. And then a kind of soft hissing sound and a sweet smell filled the room – milk was about to spill over on the stove. Mamata used the opportunity to rush away from addressing Abu Ibrahim's question; she removed the lid of the milk pot and

blew into the swollen-up milk to soothe the boiling. Abu
Ibrahim then went and stood in the balcony, and observed
evening descending upon Bailey Road. Their maidservant
had gone out, and when she returned now, Mamata set
upon her. Abu Ibrahim gazed at the light of the dying day
and heard his wife's voice, and if we looked at his face then,
we would once again be reminded of the protagonists of
Greek tragedies, who bore their fate all their lives. And if
we looked at the face of the woman on the other side, at the
other end, whose name is Mamata here, we would notice
a kind of steadfastness in the fire in her eyes and the set
of her neck, the steadfastness with which a woman builds
a family and holds together a daft husband and immature
children within the confines of that family. Mamata was
scolding their maidservant Kajoli.

'How long does it take you to go and buy something?'

The girl answered back and that was not acceptable
to Mamata.

'Don't argue with me! Once you step outside you just
don't want to come back!'

One couldn't say that Abu Ibrahim paid heed to all
this talk between his wife and the maidservant as he stood
in the veranda; he claimed that he didn't pay attention
to such things any more. He watched countless vehicles
trundling along the road beside the housing estate, he
saw the sun stooping to touch the treetops. And then he
smelled milk burning once again and heard the crash of

some metallic thing falling. Mamata now got enraged at the impossibly tiny flats on Bailey Road, and then her anger was transferred to Bindu, who happened to be standing in that small and narrow space.

'The girl's standing in this corner and putting up a show. Hey girl, Bindu—'

Abu Ibrahim turned around and saw Bindu being chased by her mother; she went to the living room and sat down on the cane chair there, bending over with her face buried in her palms, which were placed on her knees. Abu Ibrahim entered the room and pressed the switch to turn on the light. Bindu continued to sit folded up in two, Mamata began preparing food for dinner, then Abu Ibrahim once again enquired about what had happened, and when Mamata didn't reply, he went and sat next to Bindu.

'What's happened to you, Bindu?'

Like Mamata, Bindu too remained silent.

'You all right?'

Bindu didn't speak, her face was buried in her palms on her knees, her black hair was spread out on one side of her neck. Mamata heard what Abu Ibrahim said, she came forward now and complained, 'After all your pampering, she's become too audacious!'

'But tell me what happened?'

'From the moment she came back from school, she's been pestering me about going out with Soma.'

'Where to?'

'Who knows where to. She's becoming more and more mulish by the day!'

Abu Ibrahim's daughter was then about ten years old, she studied in class four in Siddheshwari School, but she looked small for her age. All the colours of tender childhood were plastered on her face, her brown skin was as soft as silk. Abu Ibrahim now recalled what Mamata had just said – that Bindu had grown up. Gazing at Bindu, he placed his hand on her head, and Bindu then began sobbing again.

'Has she eaten after coming back from school?'

'No.'

'The girl hasn't eaten since coming back from school and you're scolding her?'

'Your daughter doesn't need any scolding. I only told her that she needn't go, that's it, and then she started tormenting me.'

'Take her and give her something to eat.'

'She'll eat on her own when she's hungry, she doesn't need to be mollycoddled.'

ABU IBRAHIM MADE BINDU SIT up straight. Bindu did, but covered her face with her hands. Abu Ibrahim moved her hands away; he saw that Bindu wasn't crying, but her nostrils and lips were quivering; the corners of her eyes were wet, and her eyes were shut. Bindu's front teeth protruded a bit. When she stopped sobbing after a little while and calmed down, her teeth were visible from the gap between her lips.

'Where did you want to go?'

Bindu didn't reply, she wiped her eyes with the back of her hand and sat comfortably with her eyes shut. Abu Ibrahim gazed fondly at her face and thought, although this girl was born of Mamata's womb, she was his daughter.

'Want to go out with me?'

Bindu didn't open her eyes, she just sat there indifferently.

'Come, let me take you out for a walk. Go and eat, and then put on your sandals.'

Bindu opened her eyes and looked at Abu Ibrahim, and seeing her face he realized that Bindu was no longer a little girl who could be cajoled with sweet talk; but still he said, 'Go and eat, and then we'll go out.'

Bindu got up and put on her sandals.

'Won't you eat something? I won't go out unless you eat.'

Bindu stood there silently.

'What?'

When an expression of indifference reappeared on Bindu's face, Abu Ibrahim conceded defeat to her as well, and putting on a shirt and a pair of trousers, he went out with her. They went first to Shahbagh and rested there; he bought Bindu an ice cream. After putting the last bit of the ice cream cone into her mouth, Bindu wiped her hands on her frock.

'Why did you wipe your hands on your dress? Won't it get dirty?'

It seemed Bindu didn't hear him; she said, 'I feel *fine*.'

'What does "fine" mean?'

'"Fine" means good. Sharmin always says "fine". Sharmin's Abba also says "fine".'

'Who's Sharmin?'

'She's my friend.'

'Where did you meet her Abba?'

'At their house, they live right near our school.'

'Do you like Sharmin's Abba a lot?'

'No, he's rotten!'

'If he says, "Hey khuki, stay back in our house, I'll give you lots of ice cream, I'll give you lovely clothes," won't you stay there?'

'No!'

'Why not?'

'Won't Shubho cry?'

'What if Shubho doesn't cry?'

'No, don't I have my Abbu-Ammu at home?'

'So you have an Abbu?'

Bindu then laughed and said, 'Hmm, I do.'

'Would you like another ice cream?'

Bindu laughed. She polished off the second ice cream in a trice.

'Do you want another one?'

Bindu was hesitant. Abu Ibrahim said, 'Hey, what's up, want another one?'

'Hmm.'

'You're going to get a thrashing, a sound thrashing! If you have so much ice cream, all your teeth will fall out, you'll be toothless. Come on, get up.'

Abu Ibrahim held Bindu's hand and stood beside the road; he wanted to return home, but Bindu didn't want to go back.

'A little while later, Abbu. Can't we walk a bit more?'

Strolling with his daughter, Abu Ibrahim went past the museum and headed towards the university. Bindu followed, almost wrapping herself around his legs. The wide, black road seemed desolate but strangely beautiful under the bright lights, Abu Ibrahim liked its openness and linear drift. After walking past the public library and the art college, they halted when they came near the entrance of the university mosque; Abu Ibrahim looked at and observed the shadowy darkness inside, he thought, here's that path, here are those precincts. The clustering mango tree on the southern side of the mosque stood like a jet-black giant, and as he gazed in that direction, consciousness sprang out of his state of unconsciousness and he remembered that it was here that he had once lost himself, and here that he had once tried to find himself. He had been wrapped in this light and darkness; so many years had gone by after that, and he had distanced himself for so long from his heart. He lived in Dhaka itself now, and yet it seemed he lived very far away and could never make his way to this locality. Now he kept on losing himself; it seems that this tale of loss continued until the day he died. Bindu stood there clutching him and said, 'Come, Abbu, let's go back.'

But this time, Abu Ibrahim didn't listen to Bindu; he went with her to the front of the library building and discovered that almost everything had changed – the jamrul and lichu trees were gone, there were new buildings all around. Much of the place was unfamiliar to him, nonetheless it occurred to him that he wasn't really a stranger here; his footprints were imprinted on this library veranda, in the eerie canteen run by Madhu, and in the Arts Centre; the dust of his memory lay on this path, on the soil and on the grass, and even now the breeze wafted like a deep sigh over the grass near the palm trees in the clearing behind the library. Realizing that Bindu wasn't liking it, he put his hand on her shoulder and stood at the southern end of the long veranda of the library, as if he believed that if she felt the touch of his hand, the secret of what he was feeling would express itself to her.

'Hey Bindu!'

'Hmm?'

'Are you tired?'

'Come on, let's go back.'

'Would you like to sit here?'

'No, let's go back.'

Abu Ibrahim sat down on the edge of the veranda, his daughter standing between his knees. In front of them was the clustering koroi tree, there were groups of students; and looking in the direction of Rokeya Hall, Abu Ibrahim moved his right hand away from Bindu's shoulder and placed it on the paved floor of the veranda. But his palms only touched stony love.

'Do you know what this is?'

'Uh?'

'Do you know?'

'Which one?'

'This is the university.'

He then sat Bindu down beside him.

'This is the largest school of all.'

'Who studies here?'

'You come to study here after passing the matriculation exam and then the intermediate exam.'

'Yes, I know. Didn't you study here?'

Abu Ibrahim put his arm around Bindu, his voice turned deep.

'Yes, I used to study here.'

'Were you small then?'

'Yes, I was small then.'

'I know, you weren't even married.'

'Pfft! Who told you I wasn't married?'

'You were?'

'Yes.'

'To Ammu?'

'Yes.'

'No! You're lying.'

He couldn't win against Bindu, and she got the better of him once again; after that, they exited through the southern gate, got into a rickshaw and returned home. Mamata was teaching Shubho then. Bindu went and sat in front of them and announced that she had eaten a potato chop and two ice creams. At first Shubho chose to ignore her, then he realized that it was true and fell silent.

'Hey, why aren't you reading?'

'Bindu had two ice creams.'

'That's fine, keep quiet, read now.'

Shubho didn't want to read. Abu Ibrahim assured him, 'Read now, I'll take you out tomorrow.'

Mamata got angry on hearing that and protested, 'You've spoilt the girl already, don't spoil the boy now.'

'Don't talk rubbish!'

'Does anyone roam around until so late at night with a small girl like this?'

'I went to the university.'

'What's there? Hey boy, aren't you going to read?'

'Nothing, the two of us were just strolling around.'

Shubho stopped reading. Bindu yawned, her eyes looked drowsy. Mamata said, 'Madness!'

'What madness?'

'Is that any place to stroll around in?'

'What would you know?'

'I don't know anything at all!'

'You know so much!'

'There's always turmoil there, it's where hoodlums gather; and that's where he goes, holding a little girl's hand, for a stroll.'

Abu Ibrahim fell silent, Shubho stopped reading, and Bindu dozed. Mamata then called out to Kajoli and asked her to serve the dinner. Observing Bindu, Abu Ibrahim realized that he had made her walk too much. When he ran his hand through Bindu's hair, near her ear, she rested her head on the palm of his hand. He saw that Bindu's eyes were shut, her front teeth were sticking out, and he declared, 'I'll send Bindu to the university.'

Mamata didn't know then that none of Abu Ibrahim's dreams would be fulfilled, that all his talk would be rendered devoid of meaning, because death would arrive very swiftly and carry him away from his state of daydreaming. That's why, when Mamata heard Abu Ibrahim saying that while she was picking up Shubho's books to put them away, she pursed her lips and said, 'I know where this is coming from.'

Mamata then had a proper altercation with Abu Ibrahim that night. Following Abu Ibrahim's death,

Mamata kept remembering all these moments from the past each and every day for almost two years. After the quarrel that night, Mamata wept a lot, and when Kajoli laid out the food, Abu Ibrahim ate and then took Shubho along and went and lay down in the bedroom. Mamata stayed up without having dinner, and Bindu too stayed up with her mother. When Abu Ibrahim began to feel drowsy, he thought he heard someone's voice within his sleep, but then he realized that he wasn't asleep and the voice he had heard was Bindu's. That night, in his drowsy state, Abu Ibrahim became aware of the mysterious bond between mother and daughter. Men are never able to fathom it from the outside. He heard Bindu consoling Mamata in the adjacent room, saying, 'Ammu, Ammu,' and that night, leaving Mamata and Bindu in the next room, Abu Ibrahim fell asleep with Shubho beside him.

One thing that we may often think is that Abu Ibrahim was an unhappy man; but on some other occasion, when we see him smiling radiantly or being loving to his wife, perhaps we might think that our conclusion was not the last word. We do know that he was melancholy over a failed love, and had feelings of guilt for having strayed from the path of attaining the political ideals he had cherished in his youth. There was a girl; her name was Helen and she was his classmate, and she had been responsible for bathing him in her fire. We are aware that Abu Ibrahim maintained a diary, and if we read it, we would see a list of everything he disliked. Mamata knew about Helen, Abu Ibrahim had told her. Besides, she was in the habit of secretly reading Abu Ibrahim's diary. In an old entry from 1967, Abu Ibrahim had once described his conversation with Helen, saying that because she hadn't come to college for a few days, he had been dying to see her; after that, following Helen's return, when he went to talk to her, Abu Ibrahim felt as if his very being wanted to cease to exist, his heart was filled with pain. We don't learn whether or not Helen hurt Abu Ibrahim's feelings, but what we can infer from Abu Ibrahim's writing is that Helen did not fulfil his desires, and that he wandered around the university precincts for six years, carrying the destitution of failed love, and then sat at night in his narrow room on the second floor of Mohsin Hall, writing all these accounts in his diary. There were many books in his room in Mohsin Hall back then, and one of those books was a small collection of five essays by Mao Tse-tung. If we could retrieve this book now, which had Abu Ibrahim's name written on the first page, we would be able to leaf through the pages, and if we did that, we would see that there was a short essay in this booklet on the Canadian surgeon, Dr Norman Bethune, and at one point in the essay, Mao Tse-tung described the majesty of Dr Bethune's death by saying that some deaths were as light as a goose feather, while others were as heavy as an immovable mountain. We would observe that there was a line drawn under this sentence, in red ink, and we would at once realize that Abu Ibrahim had done that. When Abu Ibrahim died, if we remembered his thoughts regarding death from ages ago, we would find ourselves growing increasingly confused; we would fail to attach any meaning to his death. We would see him collapse into a death that was lighter and more insignificant than even a goose feather. Death was a subject Abu Ibrahim disliked very much, and the other thing he disliked was his job. He wrote many times in his diary that he did not like doing his job. But although he disliked it, he did not give it up; because despite his discomfiture, he also knew that if he did not have the job, his life would turn disastrous. And now, after having worked in the Government Secretariat for eleven years, it occurred to him yet again that this was entirely meaningless; he saw himself wasting away. He then phoned his closest colleague, Siddiq Hossain, and chatted with him.

'How are you doing?' Siddiq Hossain asked.

'Okay.'

'Are you free now? Have you finished that summary?'

'I just sent it for typing.'

'Come over, let's go for a stroll.'

Siddiq Hossain used to work in the Finance Department then; Abu Ibrahim informed his branch assistant about where he was going and left his office. Sitting in Siddiq

Hossain's office, they talked about their senior officers, like they did every day, and there was nothing complimentary there. After that, they remained silent for a while, and Abu Ibrahim noticed the krishnachura and eucalyptus trees outside the window of Siddiq Hossain's second-floor office. Mamata had once called Abu Ibrahim mad for waking her up at night to listen to the calls of flying sarus cranes. Today, Siddiq Hossain too called him mad as they sat in his office. Abu Ibrahim certainly enjoyed gazing at the red krishnachura flowers, because he remarked that the Secretariat ought to be filled with krishnachura trees. Siddiq Hossain laughed when he heard that, and blowing out a puff of smoke, he said, 'You're mad!'

'Why do you say that?'

'Because you're mad. Who are you preparing the summary for? The President?'

'For the Cabinet.'

'Has your father-in-law arrived?'

'Yes. There's no place at home, so you can imagine the situation.'

'When did he come?'

'Yesterday.'

'What's happened to him?'

'He has an inflammation of the prostate gland. He needs an operation.'

'Want some tea?'

'No, thanks.'

Siddiq Hossain rang the bell and waited for the peon, but no one came. 'There's no one,' he said. 'Everyone's gadding about, each one up to some hustle.'

'We actually work so little.'

'For what they pay us, we work too much.'

Abu Ibrahim then once again uttered his old, oft-repeated refrain, 'I don't like this job any more.'

'Come, let's go outside for a stroll.'

'Where to?'

'Just come along.'

There was a call for Abu Ibrahim on Siddiq Hossain's telephone. His Deputy Secretary wanted to know the status of the summary, and he informed him about that; he said, 'Sir, the summary is being typed, and I've also sent you two more files.' When he finished talking on the telephone, he asked Siddiq Hossain, 'All this "sir", "file", "put up" – what exactly are these, and why am I doing it?'

'You tell me.'

'I can't.'

'Are you feeling dejected?'

'I can't say.'

'Do you feel terrified thinking about the future?'

'I can't say.'

'What *can* you say?'

'I just don't like it!'

'Forget it, come, let's go for a stroll.'

'But I have some work!'

'If you don't like it then why do you worry about your work so much?'

'Because I have a wife and children, don't I?'

'Come on, we'll be back soon, half an hour at the most.'

LEAVING SIDDIQ HOSSAIN'S OFFICE, THEY got into a rickshaw and went to Motijheel, and there an incident took place, a small and trivial incident; but after that incident, Abu Ibrahim said some things so sombrely that we would think he had seen something more within the trivial nature of the incident than met the eye. Siddiq Hossain asked him to sit on the sofa outside a first-floor office in Motijheel and went inside. When Siddiq Hossain emerged after that, they went down the stairs, and Abu Ibrahim enquired, 'What work did you have here?'

'Something devious.'

Siddiq Hossain had run out of cigarettes, and the incident in question took place when they went to buy cigarettes at a shop on the pavement at the Tikatuli intersection. There was a sweet shop next to it, and in front of this shop, a beggarwoman and a small child were scraping off with their fingers and eating the sediment at the bottoms of the discarded, empty earthen bowls in which yogurt was sold. When Siddiq Hossain took out his wallet to pay for the cigarettes, the beggarwoman wiped her hand on her sari and came and stood near them, and when they turned around after paying the shopkeeper and taking the pack of cigarettes, she held out her palm in front of them.

'Mister!'

'*Maaf koro!* Excuse me.'

The woman didn't let them off, she walked along with them, almost grazing against them, and her son too walked in the vicinity of their knees. When Siddiq Hossain threatened them, the woman and her son moved away, and Siddiq Hossain and Abu Ibrahim were able to advance. But before that, Siddiq Hossain noticed that there was a yogurt stain on his trouser, just above his knee, and he cursed, 'Ei matari!'

The beggarwoman and her small child were at a loss and gaped foolishly for a few moments; after that, the child seemed to realize what he had done, and he turned around and began running, leaving his mother behind. Abu Ibrahim observed the dirty, half-naked child running like a terrified mouse and going through an open doorway, and when Siddiq Hossain chased him, Abu Ibrahim followed after. Going past a corridor, he saw the child trying to conceal himself in a corner underneath a staircase that stood in the middle. Abu Ibrahim could not figure out what Siddiq Hossain would do now, and it turned out that Siddiq Hossain too couldn't figure out what he would do. Because he stood there, gazing at the half-naked boy cowering in the corner like a thief. He didn't advance; he swore at the child, calling him a bastard, and then turned around. But then Abu Ibrahim observed that Siddiq Hossain turned back once again and advanced towards the child, he folded a five-taka note and threw it at him. We could gather that this incident became imprinted on Abu Ibrahim's mind, because immediately after that, he had an exchange with Siddiq Hossain, which the latter remembered a long time later, as he stood in front of the mosque on Bailey Square during Abu Ibrahim's namaz-e-janaza, or funerary prayer. We don't know what Abu Ibrahim made of Siddiq Hossain's conduct that day. Was he fascinated by his humanity? But we can't jump to that conclusion, because we do know that he once believed that it was not charity that was needed, rather it was a question of instituting the rights of the poor and downtrodden. But had he gradually come to think, especially after taking up this job and becoming detached from politics, that while revolution was a distant goal, this boy needed compassion at that moment, and when Siddiq Hossain displayed such kindness, did he consider him more socially useful than himself? We don't know what Abu Ibrahim surmised, and Siddiq Hossain too was unclear about that, but while returning to the Secretariat from the Tikatuli intersection by rickshaw that day, Abu Ibrahim asked him, 'May I say something?'

Siddiq Hossain laughed in surprise and said, 'Something serious?'

'Do you hate yourself?'

'Why?'

'For your way of life?'

Siddiq Hossain then asked him a difficult question, 'Do you think that there's something I should hate myself for?' Abu Ibrahim was unable to answer this question, and he said, 'Will you hate me if I change myself?'

'Do you consider yourself a god?'

Once again, Abu Ibrahim was at a loss for words, and after that he remained silent for a long time. When they got off the rickshaw and entered through Gate No. 1 of the Secretariat, it seemed Abu Ibrahim woke up from some dream and said that he was no god. Hearing him, Siddiq Hossain remarked, 'What are you saying?'

Abu Ibrahim told him nothing more. He walked towards his office. Siddiq Hossain didn't attach any importance to all this talk of his, but after Abu Ibrahim's death, as he stood in the crowd during the namaz-e-janaza, he recalled the words spoken by Abu Ibrahim a long time ago, and it occurred to him that what Abu Ibrahim had said wasn't correct. But when we get to know Abu Ibrahim, we won't be able to arrive at a conclusion as easily as Siddiq Hossain did. We'll be confused, and perhaps our confusion will persist.

Abu Ibrahim got his father-in-law, who was afflicted with a prostate problem, admitted to the Medical College hospital and had him operated upon. Because Mamata's elder brother was also around, Abu Ibrahim didn't have to

run errands that much. Yet doing even the bare minimum
made him feel feeble. Mamata was unable to visit her father
every day because they couldn't afford the daily rickshaw
fare, so she quarrelled with Abu Ibrahim about this, and
then gave him the silent treatment. Abu Ibrahim had to
perform the task of visiting his father-in-law every day, and
on most days Bindu accompanied him. Although it was a
bit far away for Bindu, they walked, and sometimes rested
on the way. Sitting at times under some champa tree in
Suhrawardy Udyan after having walked down Ramna Park,
Abu Ibrahim chatted with his daughter as they munched
peanuts. During those times, or perhaps even long before
that, he had felt that he enjoyed chatting with his daughter.
Like he had enjoyed talking to Helen in the past. She had
been his lover, and it struck him that Bindu too was his
lover. Sitting under the champa tree and talking to the
girl, he realized that there was something called love; he
became aware that when he put his hand on her head, he
himself felt assured. He then recalled something Mamata
had said about Bindu. It occurred to him that one day
when he had grown old and worn out and was in hospital
like his father-in-law, perhaps Bindu wouldn't be able to
visit him, and she would quarrel with her husband and
then weep her heart out, like Mamata did. During that
period, when Abdul Jolil Sorkar of Sirajganj town was
in Dhaka, his son-in-law, Abu Ibrahim, observed how a
father's touch enlivened a daughter, and how an old man

lived the life of his dreams once again by being reunited with his daughter. After the stitches on the surgical wound were removed, Abdul Jolil Sorkar stayed for a few days at his son-in-law's flat and that was when Abu Ibrahim discovered the nature of the relationship between father and daughter. His father-in-law and his wife reminisced about the Jamuna river; they chatted about all those days dating back to Mamata's childhood, when torrential rains poured down at Katakhali, and because there were no embankments, the rainwater overflowed the floodplain and reached their doorstep, and as they talked about the gradual demise of the Jamuna, they grieved. And thus, they relived a golden life. A life they had lived together, side by side. In between the tales, the infirm and ailing old man gazed at Mamata, and Abu Ibrahim understood the language of that gaze, he discerned a sense of lamentation in that look. The old man would rather smile and be melancholy than demand anything. After three days, he announced that he would leave. Mamata didn't want to heed him, but he did not heed Mamata's desire to not heed him; Mamata wept, but he smiled and left.

ONE EVENING THE FOLLOWING AUTUMN, while standing in the small balcony of his flat in the housing estate, Abu Ibrahim spotted the woman whom he had never wanted to encounter again; Helen was walking by with a man. He

watched her, and after that it struck him that he hadn't
seen her for a long time. He sent Bindu to fetch her. 'Ask
her, "Is your name Helen?" If she says, "Yes," then say, "My
Amma's calling you."' Mamata knew about Helen, but after
Bindu ran down, when Abu Ibrahim told Mamata about
it, she just stared at him blankly. Then there was no more
conversation between them. Mamata busied herself with
cooking, and Abu Ibrahim waited in the living room. Bindu
then arrived with Helen and the man, and stood at the flat's
door. She called out, 'Abbu.' But Abu Ibrahim remained
seated. Finally Mamata advanced, and going to the door,
she asked, 'Aapa, you're Helen aren't you?' Abu Ibrahim
then approached the door and said, 'Come inside, Helen.'

'Oh my, Ibrahim, it's you!'

'I spotted you from here and recognized you.'

That day Helen and her husband made polite
conversation, they had the nimokpara prepared by Mamata,
and took their leave. After that, Mamata returned to her
tasks, and Abu Ibrahim sat with his eyes shut. He realized,
once again, a very old truth: that he hadn't died without
Helen. He realized that he wasn't Helen's lover, he was her
devotee, and just like a goddess would, she had learnt to
disregard her devotee. That night, Mamata returned to the
subject of Helen as they lay in bed, and it occurred to Abu
Ibrahim that he knew something like this would happen.

'Why are you sulking?' Mamata asked.

'What should I do?'

Mamata then suddenly buried herself in his chest, she stroked his head and face, and kissed his lips; she held him close. Abu Ibrahim lay aslant that night, and was astonished as he planted his lips on Mamata's eyelids, because he realized that Mamata's eyes were wet. Perhaps at least this one time, Abu Ibrahim realized that there was more to his wife than her corpulence. Later, some other day, Mamata secretly read in Abu Ibrahim's diary about all his feelings that night. Abu Ibrahim had written, 'Helen came after a long time and Mamata planted the salt of love on my lips.' Two days after that, Helen came again to their flat; that day, her husband wasn't with her. Helen said hesitatingly, 'I happened to be nearby, I thought I'd come and have a chat with you people. We couldn't really talk the other day, we were in a hurry.'

The three of them sat in the living room; Mamata had an impassive face, and whenever Helen said something, she merely faked a smile. Abu Ibrahim sensed that perhaps Mamata might break into tears.

'You and your husband were abroad; when did you come back?'

'It's not been long.'

'Where are you staying now?'

'In Jayaret.'

'How do you like it?'

'It's terrible.'

When Abu Ibrahim laughed, Helen said, with the same inimitable, coy manner of the past, 'Oh no, no, don't laugh, it's true,' and as the cadence of her voice brushed against him, Abu Ibrahim sensed the trace of a missing desire awakening from amidst an imagined palm grove. Yet Abu Ibrahim laughed again, and Helen said, 'I just don't like this kind of life any more.' She frowned, there was a look of cluelessness in her eyes. Abu Ibrahim observed that Mamata's eyes were downcast; her lips gently quivering. Just then, Bindu barged into the room with springy steps, and Helen drew her close.

'Your daughter's so sweet!'

'She's a daredevil!'

'Was it you who named her?'

'Her mother did.'

'It's a beautiful name.'

'Her mother's name is Mamata.'

'Hmm, it's wonderful.'

Helen held on to Bindu.

'What will you call me, Bindu?'

Bindu laughed, she said, 'Fufu.'

'No, not Fufu, Khala.'

'Are you my Ammu's sister?'

'Yes, I'm your Ammu's Aapa.'

Bindu then exposed her big teeth and laughed, and Helen too joined her. She held Bindu in her embrace, and then she kissed her softly on her cheek. Abu Ibrahim sat silently and observed Helen's conduct, and he became confused; he couldn't make sense of all this. He liked looking at Helen; and here in Helen's arms was his daughter!

It then struck Abu Ibrahim that although he had wept a long time ago at his failure in love, he had actually not failed in anything. But at the same time, he knew that all this amounted to nothing. As the evening advanced after Helen left that day, Bindu and Shubho returned from playing downstairs, and Abu Ibrahim went and stood in the balcony. Suddenly Bindu began screaming, and Abu Ibrahim saw that Mamata had started beating her. When Abu Ibrahim went to stop her, Mamata first turned furious, and when he yelled at her, she began to weep. Abu Ibrahim understood the matter, he felt so helpless and imperilled that he became depressed. After that, he said, 'All right, if I see Helen again, I'll tell her not to come to our place.'

'I didn't say she shouldn't come, it's just that there's no need for her to put on an act with my daughter. If she comes to visit you, she ought to sit with you and then leave.'

Abu Ibrahim felt a kind of rage springing out from his depression, but he couldn't protest. Standing beside the wall inside the bedroom, Bindu sobbed, and Mamata got down to preparing dinner.

THE FRIENDSHIP THAT GREW BETWEEN Abu Ibrahim and Siddiq Hossain in the Secretariat essentially turned out to be boisterous as well as mysterious, because the two of them were poles apart. Siddiq Hossain's world was anchored in simple reasoning, and all the things he desired were within the bounds of human possibility; but when it came to Abu Ibrahim, sometimes clearly and sometimes not so clearly, it seemed that he traversed life in a continuous state of dreaminess. The two of them had a conversation one day about such matters, and we'll now hear a bit of that conversation, as well as the dialogue between Mamata and Abu Ibrahim that evening. Siddiq Hossain had canvassed for and obtained a transfer to an autonomous organization. Such organizations had immense amounts of funds and a pool of cars. Abu Ibrahim went to his office one day to meet him and asked, 'How did you wangle this?' Siddiq Hossain laughed and said, 'Do you think I'm like you!'

'Is that so?'

'It is so! What's the point of being a masochist!'

Both of them laughed again, and Siddiq Hossain asked for tea.

'Will you get a car?'

'Oh no. How can I get a personal car! Perhaps I'll be able to use the office car from time to time.'

'Any chance of going abroad?'

'Who knows, I can't tell you.'

'Something like a pre-shipment inspection?'

'Maybe.'

'In that case you'll go abroad plenty of times!'

Siddiq Hossain's peon then entered and served the tea.

'Will you treat me only to tea?'

'Come on, have it!'

'You did the right thing. I don't like being reduced to a clerk.'

'Leave your job then!'

The two of them laughed aloud again.

'You too should move over here.'

'It's no use, I can't be a manager, people aren't afraid of me.'

'There's no problem if they aren't afraid, rather it's a problem if they are; but people are actually afraid of you. Learn to love people, and they'll reciprocate.' Saying so, Siddiq Hossain began laughing again, and then Abu Ibrahim said, 'What about our promotion?'

'It should go through.'

As he was taking his leave after finishing his tea, Abu Ibrahim jested, 'You cheated me.' But that evening, when Mamata brought him some sweets on a tray, he didn't want to have them.

'I don't feel like eating.'

'Then have them later.'

Their conversation proceeded well up to this point, but it took a turn when Mamata asked, 'Has Siddiq Bhai been transferred somewhere?' Abu Ibrahim was not interested in talking about this subject, he merely said, 'Hmm…'

'Hmm what?'

Abu Ibrahim then lost his temper and burst out, 'Would you even understand if I said something?' Mamata turned silent at this humiliation, and observing that, Abu

Ibrahim felt bad. He asked her, 'Have you had the sweets?' But Mamata didn't reply. He then smiled faintly, and Mamata looked apprehensively at the smile. He remarked, 'Siddiq's such a show-off, he sent sweets to our home!' But Mamata still didn't say anything, and then Abu Ibrahim asked once again, 'Did you have the sweets?'

Mamata gave him a look. 'Cut out the act.'

'I wonder why Siddiq does all this; he overdoes things sometimes.'

'Yes, everyone should be like you!'

'Should be what like me?'

'Low-class, what else!'

That day, Abu Ibrahim had smiled somewhat cheerlessly. Mamata was perhaps joking, or perhaps it wasn't a joke; but it occurred to Abu Ibrahim that there was a complaint implied in what she said, and he knew what the complaint was all about. He then got up and went and stood in the fifteen-square-foot balcony that the estate provided – the only solace in his life. In a little while, Bindu returned from downstairs accompanied by Siddiq Hossain's younger son, Kamal.

'Ammu, can I have water?'

Bindu drank water, and Kamal stood and looked at Bindu drinking; the final drops of the water in the glass rolled into Bindu's mouth. The boy's eyes shone; looking at them, it seemed like he was imagining that Bindu was drinking nectar. After Bindu wiped her mouth with the back of her hand, Kamal said he was thirsty, and while he was drinking water, Bindu looked at him with the same eagerness. When the boy finished drinking, and he too had wiped his mouth with the back of his hand, they suddenly chortled a bit, and after that, both of them set off once again to go outside. Mamata then intervened and stopped Bindu. She said, 'Hey girl, you don't have to go out now. Kamal, you can go.' Bindu began whimpering at this unkindness on Mamata's part, and Kamal did not want to go back alone, but Mamata stood firm. She repeated, 'Go Kamal, go now and play. Bindu has work at home.'

The boy lingered for some more time, and then he said, 'Umm, I'm going,' and left. Bindu nagged, and Mamata scolded her. 'Hey, be quiet, you don't have to play so much!'

'What's all the fuss about?'

Mamata was silent.

'Why do you pick on her day and night like this?'

'A girl doesn't need to play so much! She just plays with boys all day long!'

Abu Ibrahim was amazed to hear Mamata say this and retorted, 'How old is she? What does she know of boys and girls now?' Mamata was fully aware of this liberal and modern bent of Abu Ibrahim's, so she didn't get agitated. After remaining silent for a while, she merely said with an air of finality, 'Girls don't need to play so much.'

That day, the conversation between Mamata and Abu Ibrahim didn't advance any further; it was Abu Ibrahim himself who had put that to rest, because he realized that it was futile to say any more. But for us, all these matters don't come to an end with that day; Abu Ibrahim kept picking quarrels with Mamata, and when some part of that bickering is presented before us, we'll hear it. Because we want to know about this man, Abu Ibrahim. We don't know why it's necessary for us to know about Abu Ibrahim; perhaps there's no need to know about him, or perhaps there is. Nonetheless, we'll learn and hear about him, perhaps for the sole reason that we want to read a work of fiction, and if we do that, we have to know the character or set of characters, although we know that reading and cogitation are sometimes arduous. When the three-year term of Abu Ibrahim's post in the Finance Department was completed, he was transferred to the Commerce Department where he was initially given the responsibility of the administrative branch. Owing to the greater pressure of work in this branch, Abu Ibrahim was always late returning home, and because of that Mamata's annoyance grew, and we continuously see their conversations mired in altercation. When Kajoli bought rotten fish one day, Mamata threw it away and cooked dal and potol-curry instead, and after returning from office in the evening, when Abu Ibrahim had that and said, 'I ate well,' Mamata became furious.

'So you ate well!'

'What's wrong with that?'

Mamata glared at Abu Ibrahim with her brows furrowed; she said a lot of things, but even after that it seemed she still had many more things to say. That Kajoli couldn't handle it, so Abu Ibrahim ought to go to the market; that Shubho had been coughing for the past few days, Abu Ibrahim ought to take him to the doctor; that the cane chairs were coming apart, Abu Ibrahim ought to call a carpenter immediately and get them repaired; there was so much work in a household, yet here was Abu Ibrahim, returning after spending the whole evening in the office, eating rice and potol-curry, and then declaring that he ate well! When Mamata glared at him after the harangue, Abu Ibrahim read the expression on her face, and notwithstanding his fatigue, he burst out laughing. After bursting into laughter like this another day, he told Mamata, 'I've been observing over the past few days that Bindu's always wearing a salwar; are all her bloomers torn?'

'She doesn't need to wear bloomers any more.'

Abu Ibrahim understood, he put down the newspaper he was reading, got up and went to the veranda. When Mamata came and stood beside him after a little while, he asked her, 'When will you make Bindu wear an orna?'

'Don't act smart.'

'You're turning my little girl into a woman! How old is she?'

Mamata didn't say anything; as Abu Ibrahim was calculating her age, he felt a sharp pricking pain in his back, near the spine.

'I've had a pain in my back for the last few days.'

'How come?'

'The chair in my new office is terrible; I can't sit properly on it.'

Mamata then grazed against Abu Ibrahim, and pressed her chin gently near his shoulder; it occurred to Abu Ibrahim that Mamata was always cat-like – plump, composed and lazy, demanding love by brushing against the body and legs.

'Shubho just sleeps. He's just as fluffy as you, the fatty.'

'He's jumping around the whole day, so what else will he do but sleep!'

Abu Ibrahim laughed.

'Do you want to apply balm on your back?'

'No, it's fine.'

Mamata stroked his back and asked, 'Is the pain here?'

'What's happened to you?'

'What do you mean?'

'You fondle me the moment you get a chance?'

Mamata retracted her hand and stepped aside. Abu Ibrahim laughed.

'Why are you laughing?'

Abu Ibrahim then spoke about complex feelings, in the most complicated language, the meaning of which eluded

Mamata entirely. When he finished, Mamata crossed her arms over her bosom and gazed sombrely towards some infinity in the deepening evening. Abu Ibrahim asked her, 'Want to walk down the road?'

'I don't walk on the road.'

Bindu and Shubho arrived then, and Abu Ibrahim asked Bindu, 'Want to go out?'

'Where to?'

'Just here, on the road.'

Bindu and Shubho hugged Abu Ibrahim and whooped in joy. Mamata didn't consent; she said, 'No, I won't go out.'

'Come, don't be angry.'

They left Kajoli at home and went out, and the people in the housing estate observed them walking by. Shubho and Bindu held Abu Ibrahim's two hands and they were pulling him as if they were hauling a boat ashore; Mamata fixed her anchal over her shoulder and walked a little distance away, her arms crossed over her bosom, her round face looking pleased. Abu Ibrahim felt good; he forgot about his back pain. They went past the Kakrail Mosque, and entered Ramna Park and sat on a bench under a small bokul tree. Bindu and Shubho ran in the grassy field, Shubho stumbled and fell, and Bindu then began clapping and giggling. Shubho returned to Mamata and complained, 'Bindu pushed me down.'

'Bindu didn't push you, you fell by yourself.'

'No, Bindu pushed me!'

Mamata brushed away the grass on Shubho's body; Abu Ibrahim gestured to the ice-cream seller and bought ice cream; the children were overjoyed.

'Will you have one?'

Mamata guffawed.

'Why don't you have one, Ammu!'

'You have it, girl.'

'Then have a bite from mine!'

Bindu brought her ice cream towards Mamata, who feigned anger, saying, 'God, what a girl she is!'

'Abbu, do you want a bite?'

'Will you give me one?'

Scraping off a bit of ice near the top of the ice cream with a bite, Abu Ibrahim said, *'Fine, thank you!'* Bindu bared her big teeth and laughed, and then Abu Ibrahim said to Shubho, 'Will you give me a bite too?' Standing near Mamata's lap, Shubho hesitated, and then he held out his ice cream towards Abu Ibrahim. But Abu Ibrahim didn't take it, and Shubho took back his hand and continued eating the ice cream.

'He's a greedy ogre,' Bindu said.

Shubho looked at Bindu with a vulnerable gaze.

'But Abbu didn't have any!'

'"Didn't have any!" Selfish ogre!'

Shubho got angry. 'Look at her, Ammu!'

Then they got up and walked in the park; they enjoyed
themselves. As they walked past a bed of marigold flowers,
Shubho wanted to pluck one. Abu Ibrahim saw that the
plants were in a poor state. People had plucked out all the
flowers. He found a small one and plucked it for Shubho,
who smelled it and then put it into the chest-pocket of his
shirt, and then they continued walking. A man came and
stood in front of them; he was wearing a khaki-coloured
shirt over a lungi. 'Why did you pluck the flower?' Abu
Ibrahim realized that the man had been nearby; he said,
'It's a dry flower; my son was asking for it.'

'Should you pluck it just because he was asking for it?'

Abu Ibrahim stood solemnly with his wife and
children.

'So what do you want me to do now?'

'Why are you showing me your temper?'

'How am I showing my temper?'

'First you pluck a flower, and then you show your
temper!'

Abu Ibrahim then lost his cool. 'Look, miya, don't
complicate matters; I plucked your flower, tell me what
you're going to do now!'

'Plucking flowers is prohibited, didn't you see the
notice?'

Abu Ibrahim sized up the man properly; he was a
middle-aged, wasted-looking, skinny man. Abu Ibrahim
couldn't figure out whether he was extraordinarily dutiful

or an extraordinary rascal. Another gardener wearing a khaki shirt then arrived, and after hearing everything, he resolved the matter. Abu Ibrahim snapped, 'There's no more than ten flowers in the entire park, but now it's a calamity because of this one!'

They began to walk again. Mamata then moved ahead, took out the flower from Shubho's pocket and flung it away, saying, 'It's a rubbish flower, throw it away!' While returning by rickshaw, Abu Ibrahim observed a dark shadow on Mamata's face; he asked, 'What?'

'Everyone plucks flowers; there isn't a single one left, and yet what kind of behaviour was that, just for a small flower!'

With his eyes cast on the road, Abu Ibrahim said, 'I know it's unreasonable, but if the man had said one more word, I would have punched him!'

ONE DAY, AROUND THE SAME time, Helen phoned Abu Ibrahim at his office.

'I thought you might have left the country!'

'It's almost time to leave. I don't like it at all.'

'But everyone wants to go abroad.'

'They do, but once they go, they lament.'

Helen then told him that, the following Friday, they were going for an outing to the National Park in Chandra, and she invited Abu Ibrahim to come along with them.

'Will you come?'

'I have to think about it.'

'There's nothing to think about; we'll pick you all up by nine in the morning.'

'All of us?'

'You, your wife, and definitely Bindu.'

'I also have a son, Shubho.'

'Yes, Shubho too; I'm sorry.'

'How will so many people fit in the car?'

'It's not a problem, we'll get a micro-bus.'

'Will we have lunch in the woods?'

'Maybe.'

'Can I contribute?'

'No.'

'All right, let me ask Mamata and see.'

'Ask her; but you have to come.'

MAMATA WAS FULL OF CONSTERNATION when she heard about the outing plan, and she snorted, 'What a hassle!' Abu Ibrahim tried to remain as impassive as possible, he didn't protest, but he also abstained from indulging her unwillingness; and in this way, the following Friday arrived. But waking up that day to drizzling rain, even Mamata felt dejected. Then, at around nine in the morning, the untimely rain ceased, and about an hour later, Helen and her squad arrived by micro-bus, and parked at the clearing in front

of Building No. 11. After that, as they sped along Minto
Road and past the Sheraton Hotel, they could see bright
sunshine in the sky.

They stopped the car near a clump of gojari trees
and spread out in a shady clearing of grass in Chandra
National Park. Abu Ibrahim counted fourteen people
in all, including the driver; among them was Helen's
husband, his two friends, and their wives and children.
He went and sat down on the grass at a clean spot in the
shade of a tree, and the others followed him. The men
in the group then began chattering, while the women
sat and listened quietly, with their children beside them.
They talked about the developed countries in the West
and about the lives of Bengali folk in all those countries;
they had an elaborate discussion comparing their country
with foreign lands, and they reached the conclusion that it
was only by going abroad that one developed feelings for
one's country and discovered a love for one's homeland in
one's heart. After that, they moved to the subject of their
country's politics and talked about the role of the CIA
in the assassination of Sheikh Mujibur Rahman. They
declared that Henry Kissinger had mentioned that he had
disliked two people. One of them was Salvador Allende,
and the other was Sheikh Mujibur Rahman, and both of
them were murdered by the military of their respective
countries. Citing an English-language book by Lawrence
Lifschultz titled *The Unfinished Revolution*, they argued that

the American embassy in Dhaka had known that Sheikh
Mujib would be assassinated. While they were discussing
Lifschultz's book, they didn't notice that their wives and
children had moved away and started another gathering.
After a while, Abu Ibrahim gazed lazily at the womenfolk
standing far away; they appeared to him like four butterflies
flitting about in the green grass. The wife of one of Helen's
husband's friends was exceptionally beautiful; she laughed
as she spoke, and seeing that from afar, Abu Ibrahim
was entranced. He observed that Mamata, with her arms
crossed over her bosom, was trying to say something. In
fact, looking at Mamata clad in her ghee-coloured silk
sari with green prints, he was reminded of a plump moth.
And Helen was so dolled up that Abu Ibrahim's eyes were
scorched when he looked at her, the movements of her
arms emerging from a red sleeveless blouse flashed like
lightning in the pupils of his eyes. Helen's husband then
began talking about the birth of music, and the women in
the group once again moved towards the menfolk while
their five children continued playing gollarchut at a little
distance. And in this way, all of them gradually became
tired, and after a while their conversation came to a stop,
and each one of them gazed silently in various directions,
and after that the womenfolk got up again and went and
stood afar. Abu Ibrahim observed that a leaf fell from a
gojari tree and descended towards Helen's head, and when
she raised her hand to catch the detached yellow leaf,

beneath her sari, her blouse-sheathed breast flashed like a
radiant orb before his eyes, and Helen then became aware
that Abu Ibrahim was looking at her. She advanced towards
him and said, 'Come, let's go for a walk, all right?'

Needless to say, Abu Ibrahim had no prior mental
preparation for that day's events, he had not hoped for
anything; it just seemed as if something splendid had
expressed itself in his life at the wrong time, which would
then disappear once again like a dream, and Abu Ibrahim
was unable to come up with an explanation for all these
events in his lifetime. When Helen suggested going for
a walk, Abu Ibrahim agreed, and in front of everyone
they walked away together through the sunlight and the
shade. At first, they kept walking, they walked through
many vacant places and many clumps of gojari trees, and
then they realized that they had fallen silent. And thus,
amidst that silence, they advanced. Abu Ibrahim's gaze
was fixed on the tree ahead and on the sky, while Helen's
eyes were trained on the red dust on the path. They left the
walking trail and went up a mound, and then sat down at
a spot. With her eyes fixed on the earth, Helen tilted her
neck and smiled, and Abu Ibrahim did not know why she
was smiling. He stretched his legs out in front, rested his
hands on the earth behind him and sat gazing at the sky
with his brows furrowed, and Helen had no idea what he
was looking for in the void of the sky. She sat with her
arms around her folded knees, the sole of her left foot lay

touching Abu Ibrahim's trousers over his knee. She covered herself with her anchal, and her blood-red ruby earring dangled like the forbidden fruit close to Abu Ibrahim's face. They sat like that for a while, and after that they stood up, within touching distance from one another. Abu Ibrahim then heard Helen whispering, 'I don't like it, Ibrahim,' and then Abu Ibrahim said in a low voice, 'Come, let's walk.'

When Abu Ibrahim and Helen returned to the group still sitting in the shade of the gojari trees, it was two o'clock, and Helen said, 'We didn't realize how far we'd walked.'

Abu Ibrahim did not learn immediately about what happened to Helen that day after returning from Chandra. But it caused a storm in his own family. That night, Mamata slept with her face turned towards the wall, and didn't say a word to Abu Ibrahim when she woke up the next morning. Abu Ibrahim had breakfast and left for his office. After that, at around ten in the morning, Siddiq Hossain telephoned him.

'Are you in your room? I'm coming down.'

Siddiq Hossain arrived within five minutes. Abu Ibrahim said, 'Have some tea.'

'No, come, let's go to the Housing Directorate, let's get the application forms for the plots in Rupnagar.'

'Where's the money to buy land?'

Without wasting any time pondering over Abu Ibrahim's question, the two of them went to the Housing Directorate, paid ten taka and obtained two application forms and prospectuses. Going through the prospectus as they sat in Abu Ibrahim's office, they learnt that the price of a two-and-a-half kattha plot of land was forty thousand taka, and an advance of five thousand had to be paid together with the application form; the price of a five kattha plot was sixty thousand taka, and the advance to be paid was ten thousand. Abu Ibrahim knew even then that he wouldn't buy a plot, nonetheless he said to Siddiq Hossain, 'Two-and-a-half katthas will be enough for me.' Siddiq Hossain too said that he would take a two-and-a-half kattha plot, and after that he left. The senior officer in the administrative section of Abu Ibrahim's department then telephoned him and called him over; he informed him that arrangements were being made for his transfer to a new section. Abu Ibrahim protested, but he realized that it wouldn't work; on the way back home, he said to Siddiq Hossain, 'This new section is full of trouble, it will be the death of me.'

'What kind of trouble?'

'All the trouble of the country. Everyone comes and creates a ruckus here!'

'Beautiful!' exclaimed Siddiq Hossain and whistled, 'Learn to love people.'

'Is that so?'

'Yes. Life is about giving and receiving love.'

Their car then reached the housing estate, and after he climbed up the stairs to his flat, it occurred to Abu Ibrahim that he was trapped in a cage like a mouse, because when he sat down for dinner, Mamata didn't come and sit with him; she had stopped talking to Abu Ibrahim. When he tried to talk about the matter, she said that she could never sit and eat with a man of his character, and that she would go back to Sirajganj. Out of a kind of helplessness, Abu Ibrahim became furious, and as a result, the matter remained unresolved, and the next day, when he returned from office, he found that Mamata had left with Shubho and Bindu.

ABU IBRAHIM DIDN'T ACT AT once to bring Mamata back. He spent the next few days quietly; he joined the new section, and on Siddiq Hossain's insistence, he filled up the application for the plot of land in Rupnagar, and considered drawing five thousand taka from his provident fund savings for the advance. He thought that Mamata would return of her own accord, but when a week went by and she didn't come back, he took leave for four days and went to Sirajganj. In his in-laws' house there, after dinner, his father-in-law said to him, 'My daughter's crazy; I'm happy that you came to take her back.' Abu Ibrahim then gazed at Mamata's silent face; he remembered Helen, who was left behind in Dhaka. But Abu Ibrahim realized that he could not carry on without Mamata, and the next day he set out with his wife and children for his ancestral house in Boikunthopur. Mamata and Shubho climbed into a bullock cart, while Bindu walked a bit of the way with him. Going through the town, the bullock cart crossed a dry canal, took the road on the right side of Bahirgola rail station, and headed westwards along the mud road. After proceeding eight miles, when the bullock cart came to a stop at his ancestral house in Boikunthopur, it was past noon. Abu Ibrahim and his family spent two nights and a day there. Because of their sudden arrival on this day in late-Poush, not long after the harvest, there was exuberance in the house, and a kind of festive spirit prevailed; but even within the festivity, as his elderly father expressed his joy at their presence, he also mentioned the crop loss, he spoke about the growing infertility of the soil, and their relentless failure in sustaining their way of life. His ailing father trained his uncertain, lacklustre eyes on him, and taking his emaciated arm out of the shawl he was draped in, he gestured in the air, 'It's extremely difficult to survive!' His mother looked timidly at him; he studied her face and it occurred to him that her nose ring looked larger than before, and that she had become frailer and smaller. His two younger brothers came, and their wives stood silently nearby with ghomtas drawn over their heads. Abu Ibrahim felt a stab of depression, he thought his life was devoid of ascent, because his identity and all his roots lay in a darkness in Boikunthopur that was almost beyond remedy, and it seemed like he had no power at all to help in illuminating it. Amidst all that gloom, he cheerily declared, 'I want to eat pitha, Ma, I want pitha, make pitha.' After that, sitting that night atop a haystack made from new paddy, with a wood fire burning in the middle of the inner courtyard, the men of the house chattered, while the womenfolk pounded rice in the threshing room by the light of the lantern. From having slept several nights on a bed laid out on the raised platform in the south-facing loft under the charchala or four-sided roof, Abu Ibrahim realized that straw had been spread out under his bedding to make it soft; the petrichor fragrance of the new straw overwhelmed him. And when Mamata lay down, Abu Ibrahim, immersed in the fragrance of new grain and the love of a woman's body, spoke about many things, and after a while he informed Mamata about the application for a plot of land in Rupnagar. He did that because he was aware that Mamata's spoken and unspoken yearning was to own a bit of land in Dhaka, to build a tiny home. Mamata kept in mind this talk of buying land, and when they returned to Sirajganj a day later, Abu Ibrahim's father-in-law asked him at night, 'Why do you want to buy land?'

Abu Ibrahim figured out the matter, and said, 'No, I'm just putting in an application.'

'Where's the place?'

'It's Rupnagar, in Mirpur.'

'How much land? What's the price?'

'It's a two-and-a-half kattha plot, it costs forty thousand taka. An advance of five thousand taka has to be paid with the application.'

'That's good, submit the application. Don't be a wanderer like this.'

'It won't come through, it's pointless.'

'What's wrong with giving it a try! Do you have the money? Have you submitted the application?'

'No, I haven't, but I'll do it soon.'

Abu Ibrahim's father-in-law then said to him that, after all, they were family, and he offered Abu Ibrahim some money to take back with him. Abu Ibrahim didn't consent to that; he told his father-in-law that he would let him know if he needed money.

Five or six days after returning to Dhaka, Helen phoned him at his office and asked him how he was.

'I'm fine,' Abu Ibrahim replied.

'It's almost time for us to leave.'

'Why don't you drop by my office one day?'

'Why your office?'

'It's convenient to talk here.'

'I might come down one day.'

'Phone me beforehand to let me know, I'll bring you in from the gate.'

'How about today?'

'Now?'

'Yes.'

Abu Ibrahim showed the entry pass and escorted her to his room, and after that when the half-day ended at two, they left and went and sat in a secluded corner of a seedy Chinese restaurant. They were almost unable to say anything, and had vegetable soup and prawn balls in silence. Abu Ibrahim noticed that Helen no longer had red rubies on her ears; instead, there were small pearl studs set in gold.

'Why aren't you saying anything?'

He looked at Helen's face; he thought that he had innumerable things to say to her, but they did not merit uttering now. When the soup bowl was empty, he looked once again at Helen, and after gazing at her for a little while, he asked her, 'Will you come along with me one day to this place?'

'Which place?'

'A friend's flat.'

'What's there?'

'Nothing, just asking; the two of us can sit and talk there in peace.'

'Doesn't your friend have a family?'

'He didn't marry.'

'Where does he live?'

'In Mohammadpur; will you come?'

Helen paused for a long while, and after that she said, 'I will.'

'I'll take you there.'

'Mohammadpur is close to my place. Give me the address, I'll get there on my own.'

Inside the dimly lit Chinese restaurant, because of Abu Ibrahim's ignorance regarding the extent of a woman's mysteriousness, the preface to his subsequent fall had begun to be scripted; but he had no clue about it. He asked Helen, 'When will you come? Next Friday?'

'All right. What time will you be there?'

'Around ten.'

'Okay.'

SINCE ABU IBRAHIM WAS LATE in withdrawing money from his provident fund, Siddiq Hossain lent him the cash, and he submitted his application with that. Siddiq Hossain too genuinely wanted Abu Ibrahim to own a bit of land in Dhaka – perhaps he liked him for some reason; although we know that Abu Ibrahim eventually did not buy a plot in Rupnagar, rather, very soon, his dead body departed Dhaka for Sirajganj. After applying for plots in Rupnagar, the two of them went one day to view the site of the Rupnagar housing project, located on the fringes of Mirpur, and then Abu Ibrahim became preoccupied in his new section, and one day during this time, despite his busy schedule and cold demeanour, a man gradually advanced towards him; we could call the man Khaled Jamil. Mamata too became acquainted with him subsequently. He called on Abu Ibrahim on two consecutive days, asking for an extension of the time limit pertaining to two import shipments; he was tall and good-looking, he talked a lot, and as he spoke, he switched from Bangla to English. He came again one day, puffing on a cigarette, and said, 'Let's have some tea, sir!' When Abu Ibrahim arranged for tea out of courtesy, he joked, 'I took advantage of you!' Abu Ibrahim had to laugh when he heard that, and say, 'Oh, it's nothing!' Khaled Jamil whispered, 'Sir, some souvenirs are given as gifts from our firm, next time I will be honoured to include you in the list.'

Abu Ibrahim laughed and said, 'It's not necessary.'

'Of course not, but sir…' Khaled Jamil lit another cigarette and changed the subject. He asked, 'Sir, it's sad that you don't smoke. Actually, I have no hesitation in telling you, we're friends. I have some good friends like you, and I have some important relatives also. Our business, well I have no hesitation in telling you about it – after all, you know the nature of the business. We earn it at no cost, we get a commission, we keep a part of that, and we share the other part with our friends.'

Abu Ibrahim laughed again when Khaled Jamil said all that, and he replied, 'I know.'

'Have a cigarette.'

'No, thanks. I don't smoke.'

'That's good; I have to go now.' Saying so, he got up and left, and the day after Abu Ibrahim had vegetable soup with Helen in a Chinese restaurant, Khaled Jamil showed up once again.

'I came for some work, sir.'

'What kind of work?'

'It's all good, totally clean.'

Khaled Jamil then told him what the matter was; he explained that the Trading Corporation of Bangladesh was looking to import five thousand tons of aluminium ingots. TCB needed an additional allocation for that from the foreign loan assistance fund, and so it would be good if that allocation was made from the foreign grant assistance. Abu Ibrahim then frankly explained to Khaled Jamil the situation regarding that year's allocation for commodity loan assistance. He told him, 'All the funds under the foreign grant assistance have been allocated. There's nothing left for any new allocation.'

'I know, sir,' Khaled Jamil responded. 'All that's needed is for you to write to the overseas resources office to arrange for additional allocation from the foreign grant assistance, as requested by TCB.'

'But TCB hasn't written to us.'

'You'll get the letter by tomorrow.'

He received the letter from TCB the following day, and Khaled Jamil arrived a short while after that.

'This is a completely clean case, sir.'

'But why didn't they notify us about the aluminium ingot requirement when they drew the allocation at the beginning of the year?'

'There was no requirement then, but now they think they need the ingots. Haven't they mentioned that in the letter?'

There wasn't really anything Abu Ibrahim and his ministry could do; in the light of TCB's requirement, a letter was written to the overseas resources office asking for the requested additional fund allocation to be arranged, and on Thursday afternoon Khaled Jamil arrived at his office and asked, 'How are you, bhai?' And then he added, 'No, it's not that matter. I had some other work nearby, so I thought I'd come over and look you up.'

'I see. How are you?'

'I'm fine. Are you doing well?'

Abu Ibrahim smiled and said, 'How are your other businesses running?'

'Businesses don't run by themselves, you know, they have to be run.'

'How's the running going then?'

'I'm trying, but is that enough! Given the situation in the country.'

'Why, what's happened in the country?'

'Are you saying that everything is positive?'

'I didn't say that.'

'Then?'

As Abu Ibrahim looked in his direction, the man continued, 'There are no rules here, no discipline.'

Abu Ibrahim remained silent, hoping that by doing so the man would be done with the subject and leave; but Khaled Jamil didn't get up, he carried on, 'There might be martial law.'

'Do you think so?'

'Read the papers ... No, the generals aren't happy.'

Abu Ibrahim fell silent once again, and Khaled Jamil said, 'Let's have some tea, please call your peon.'

Abu Ibrahim was irked, and one could say that the display of such extreme familiarity by the man made him a bit angry too. Before he could stop him, Khaled Jamil rang the bell and called the peon, and took out his wallet from his pocket. He then said, 'Please don't mind; I haven't had breakfast this morning, let me order some breakfast.'

Abu Ibrahim understood the matter clearly, he looked helplessly at Khaled Jamil, and then he said that he didn't want to have anything other than tea.

Khaled Jamil then acceded to Abu Ibrahim and gave the peon money for tea alone. Observing this conduct on the part of Khaled Jamil, perhaps we might think that he was overcome in the face of the firmness of Abu Ibrahim's resolve, but subsequently we'll learn about various incidents which will lead us to think that in these preliminary days, Khaled Jamil was toying with Abu Ibrahim, like with an unaccustomed and reluctant fish that found itself on land. As Abu Ibrahim sipped the tea, he said, 'You've been running around for the fund allocation, so are you getting the order for the supply of the ingots?'

'I might get it.'

'Which country will it arrive from?'

'From our principal's country, Sweden.'

'Do they need to clear out their warehouse?'

'Maybe, but TCB requires the item.'

After Khaled Jamil left that day, Abu Ibrahim was idle for a while, and so he remembered Helen. 'I'll see you tomorrow at Kamal's flat,' he muttered. He was somewhat amazed at his soliloquy, and so, shedding the veil of timidity, he asked himself what he really wanted, and it occurred to him that he didn't know the answer. When he returned home in Siddiq Hossain's car after two o'clock that day, he seemed a bit preoccupied, and after that, when he went and stood in the balcony of his flat that evening, he wondered once again what he wanted from Helen, and he told himself, 'I don't know.' But as he stood amidst the fresh darkness of dusk, Abu Ibrahim realized that he couldn't excuse himself, and once again the question presented itself, of what he wanted to do with Helen when he would be alone with her tomorrow in Kamal's flat. And then it occurred to him that he actually knew his plan; standing in the misty darkness, without uttering a word, he silently thought to himself, 'I'll strip you naked.' Abu

Ibrahim realized that he had known this from the time he had asked Helen to come to Kamal's flat. But now, with only the space of a night before the ensuing event, when he laid this truth bare to himself, he found that his heart was filled with a kind of anguish; and Abu Ibrahim went to sleep that night with that anguish. When he woke up in the morning, he sat in front of the television, and in this way, once it was past ten and it was approaching eleven, with his eyes fixed on the television screen, and without making any sound, he kept telling Helen, 'Go back today, Helen, people have to go back like this at times, all alone, dejected and bent, go back today.' But as he sat in front of the television that day, Abu Ibrahim didn't know the truth that life was always merely a game of joy and pain. Because when he went to the office the next day, Kamal phoned him and swore at him roundly for having made him wait unnecessarily in his flat on Friday morning. When he thus learnt from Kamal that Helen too hadn't gone to the flat, at first he felt like laughing, but after that he became dejected. We observe Abu Ibrahim's life becoming untethered in this way, and gradually the truth dawns on us that there was no end to his fall. Sitting in front of the television, Abu Ibrahim had, as if repudiating Helen, asked her to go back; but Helen hadn't even shown up. In fact, within three to four days, he realized that just as he himself had a plan when he asked Helen to come to Kamal's flat as they sat in the Chinese restaurant, Helen too had known, even as she consented to the proposal, that she wouldn't go. Because shortly afterwards, Abu Ibrahim received a letter from Helen at his office address, and from that he learnt that Helen's flight had in fact been on Wednesday night, two days before Friday, and that they had left the country when they took that flight. Helen wrote in her letter, 'I never intended to hurt you, Ibrahim.' Abu Ibrahim realized that there was nothing he could do, and after that, for a few days, he once again seemed like all those Greek characters who were afflicted by destiny and went around bearing that fate. In this regard, we would assume that Khaled Jamil too appeared in Abu Ibrahim's life like another agent of fate, and he was in fact operative until the day Abu Ibrahim died. One evening, as Abu Ibrahim was walking back home after buying groceries at the market in Shantinagar, he bumped into Khaled Jamil. He insisted that Abu Ibrahim get into his car, and he dropped him in front of his building. Out of courtesy then, Abu Ibrahim had to say, 'Please come in and have a cup of tea,' and Khaled Jamil acceded to the request without any hesitation. From what Abu Ibrahim wrote in his diary that night, we learn that Khaled Jamil's behaviour had at first seemed comical to him. But after that, when he gazed at his unblemished, urbane face, he could not discern any deficiency or inconsistency there. He didn't spot any lapse in his limpid personality. While he was having tea and salty biscuits with Khaled Jamil in the sitting room that day, a man arrived. When he rang the bell, Abu Ibrahim opened the door; Mujibur Rahman was standing at the entrance with a grim face, and he had a packet of sweets in his hand. He stammered as he looked at Abu Ibrahim's crestfallen face. Abu Ibrahim could only gather that he had brought the packet of sweets for his children. It took a few minutes for Abu Ibrahim to arrive at a decision; he sent Mujibur Rahman away, and when he returned to the room, Khaled Jamil asked him, 'What happened?'

'It was someone who lost his job, he's appealed to the ministry to get it back.'

'What had he done?'

'The stocks in the warehouse didn't reconcile.'

'What will you do?'

'The matter is being examined.'

Khaled Jamil then remarked, 'Such cases are extremely sensitive, because there's a human element associated with them.'

Abu Ibrahim suddenly got annoyed, perhaps he was ill at ease inwardly after observing Mujibur Rahman plodding away along the road of the housing estate like an expelled and dejected shadow. He said, 'I can't figure out whether you're trying to give me some kind of a lesson!'

Khaled Jamil turned grave when he heard that. He lit a cigarette, and said, 'You don't understand me. I only want to be easy and lucid with you people. I know many young and bright officers like you. I am a businessman; so naturally, my life is difficult and challenging. I have a relationship with you, even if it's a distant one. It's like a game – you'll play according to your deliberation, that's agreed. But sometimes ... well let's say everyone on the table is drinking alcohol, and then if one person has soft drinks, it creates a kind of unexplained inconvenience.'

Abu Ibrahim said, 'I'm sorry. But since you display a kind of a well-intentioned attitude towards me, I think there has to be a reason for that.'

'Yes, because we can be friends. But we can't be friends if you drink Fanta while I drink whisky.'

'Why can't you also drink Fanta?'

Khaled Jamil laughed. They figured out that there was no likelihood of being in agreement on such matters. But as Khaled Jamil was leaving, he remarked, 'Life's not like drinking Fanta, it's like a hard drink,' and Abu Ibrahim let him leave without adding anything more. Entering the bedroom, Abu Ibrahim found Mamata sitting on the bed and stitching on a piece of cloth that resembled a kantha.

'What's the matter?' he asked with a laugh.

'What?'

'You're stitching a baby-kantha! What's up?'

'Not funny!'

Abu Ibrahim turned serious and said, 'What is this?'

'A cover for the dressing table.'

'What kind of cover is this?'

'The kind it ought to be.'

Abu Ibrahim then laughed again, and said, 'Let me tell you something.'

Mamata looked at Abu Ibrahim.

'Bindu and Shubho are growing up.'

'So, what of it?'

'We can have another baby.'

'Don't talk rubbish.'

'What else do you need this huge body of yours for?'

Mamata didn't say any more. Abu Ibrahim went and sat in the living room, and Kajoli made him a cup of tea. Mamata then entered the room, holding the cloth she was stitching.

'Have you heard from Helen?'

'They've left.'

'Didn't she come to meet you at home?'

'Maybe she's scared of you.'

After that, the two of them were silent for a while, and then Mamata asked, 'Are you scared of me too?'

Abu Ibrahim looked dejectedly at Mamata and observed that the woman in front of him was like the fabric of the evolving day, cast in light and shade. He saw that Mamata had her back and head flat against the wall, a shadow flitted across her face, and her eyes were brimming with tears. That day, for those few moments, Abu Ibrahim was rendered speechless, and after that when Mamata wiped away her tears, he got up and went and stood in his favourite spot, the balcony. Mamata's tears overwhelmed him, and then one day Khaled Jamil arrived at his office and said, 'I came to invite you over for a Fanta; my principal has arrived from Sweden, and so a dinner has been organized next Sunday at the Sheraton, and you are cordially invited to it.' Abu Ibrahim declined, and after a few days Khaled Jamil returned and said, 'You didn't come. We missed you very much!' Abu Ibrahim laughed somewhat shyly, he sent for tea and declared, 'Only tea.' Khaled Jamil suddenly turned gleeful at that and said, 'Only tea! Simplicity is greatness and greatness is simplicity, you are both simple and great!' When Abu Ibrahim laughed, Khaled Jamil let him be immersed in laughter and waited. After that, when Abu Ibrahim had regained his composure, he disclosed the work he had come for: 'A proposal for the purchase of cement is coming up for your approval.'

'Is that why you are so exuberant?'

'No, it's not that.'

Khaled Jamil then explained that he did not want any undue favour from Abu Ibrahim. He wouldn't ask him to do anything untoward. He only wanted due consideration and goodwill. And saying that he would come again, he left. After Khaled Jamil left, Siddiq Hossain came to Abu Ibrahim's room and took him along to the Directorate of Housing; they returned home after that. That night, there was a military coup in the country; waking up in the morning, people in the housing estate heard the news on the radio about the declaration of martial law and the imposition of curfew in the city. The elderly and contrite man who had been elected president of the country was removed, and in the evening, everyone listened to the speech of the uniformed, handsome and young Chief Martial Law Administrator on television. Two days later, when daytime curfew was lifted and offices opened once again, Abu Ibrahim went to his office, and around half past one in the afternoon, when the day's mail arrived, it included the letter regarding the purchase of cement. Siddiq Hossain arrived a little later, and they headed home. He remarked, 'So you've become a landowner.'

'Is that so? Who told you?'

'I had gone to find out. Your name has come up in the lottery.'

'And yours?'

'Mine too.'

'Fantastic!'

After Abu Ibrahim had lunch at home, he went out again, and when he returned in the evening, he found that Mamata had gone to Siddiq Hossain's flat, taking Shubho along. He spent the entire evening chattering with Bindu, and then seeing that Mamata and Shubho hadn't yet returned, the two of them went out, leaving Kajoli at home. They felt a mild breeze blowing over the road in front of the housing estate and across the playfield.

'Isn't the breeze lovely, Abbu?'

'Hmm.'

'It's so hot inside the house!'

'Hmm. Want to go for a bit of a stroll down the road?'

'Yes.'

They advanced and halted at the main road, and then Abu Ibrahim retracted his suggestion of going for a stroll; he said, 'Let it be for today. We'll go another day.' Bindu felt disheartened. She went and sat on the edge of the pavement in the shadow of a teak tree.

'Can we sit here for a while, Abbu?'

'Of course not, how can one sit on the pavement?'

Bindu pleaded, 'It's such a *fine* breeze, Abbu, let's sit here. After all, Ammu and Shubho will come this way,' and saying so, she got up, held Abu Ibrahim's hand and took him towards the dark spot under the teak tree.

'When you see Ammu and Shubho coming, be quiet, don't say anything.'

'Why?'

'I'll scare them from behind.'

'What if your Ammu screams?'

'It's Shubho who will scream.'

'How are all your friends at school?'

'They're doing well.'

'What are their names again?'

'Sonia, Piyu and Iffat. Do you know Abbu, Piyu had gone with her folks to India on holiday? Her Ammu brought back lots of beautiful saris.'

'Do you want a sari?'

'Yes, but will you get me one?'

'Very well then, I'll get you one. I'll dress you in a sari and send you off to your in-laws' house.'

'Hah!'

'Hah what?'

Bindu didn't answer, and then it occurred to Abu Ibrahim that his daughter would be the sweetest wife in the whole world; she would light up a home and overwhelm a man's life; and there was a gust of wind, and when Bindu shivered a bit, Abu Ibrahim draped his arm around her and drew her close. One of Bindu's hands was wrapped in Abu Ibrahim's. Her fingers played with his, and he could smell the scent of dried perspiration from her hair. After sitting in this manner for a long time, they spotted Mamata and Shubho approaching from afar, and although they were sitting in the shadowy darkness, Shubho noticed them. Mamata reproached Abu Ibrahim for sitting like that on the pavement with his daughter. Bindu held Mamata's hand and pulled her down; Mamata sat down for a moment, and then stood up again, saying, 'No, let's go, Kajoli's all alone at home.' Mamata's resolve let Bindu and Shubho down, and when Abu Ibrahim didn't come to their aid either, they had to return home. Bindu and Shubho walked clasping Abu Ibrahim's hands tightly, but once they reached the road inside the housing estate, they let go and ran, and as they turned around when they neared their building, through the gap between the tall buildings of the estate, the boy and girl saw a sparkling moon floating in the sky.

'Gosh! Look, Abbu, what a huge moon!'

Abu Ibrahim looked, and it seemed to him that the orb of light visible above the cornice of Building No. 10 was about to tumble down right there.

'Look, Mamata!'

Mamata glanced upwards and then turned her face away.

'Look, the moon resembles you!'

'Don't play the fool!'

'Come, let's sit down here for a bit.'

Bindu and Shubho were thrilled at Abu Ibrahim's suggestion. But Mamata wasn't pleased. They sat down beside the road in front of their building; Mamata stood like a schoolteacher with her hands crossed over her bosom. Abu Ibrahim observed that Kajoli was standing at the window of their flat; he pointed her out to Bindu. Bindu waved her hands and called out, 'Kajoli, hey Kajoli, there's the moon!'

'They've all gone crazy,' Mamata complained, and Abu Ibrahim echoed, 'It's because the moonlight's enchanting!'

'Come on, get up everyone!'

But no one listened to Mamata, so she left them behind and went upstairs. That night, when Abu Ibrahim lay down after Bindu and Shubho had fallen asleep, Mamata parted the curtains on the window and let the moonlight slip in through the opening and fall on the bed as she sat gazing at him, her back turned to the moon.

'You can almost feel the moonlight tonight on your skin,' Mamata muttered, and after that she lay down on her side, and it appeared as if a tide of moonlight came surging from behind her, crossed her and spilled over the bed.

'Have you thought about the money for the plot?'

'Let's see what can be done.'

'Shall I write to Abba?'

'Let me first see what the situation is.'

Mamata paused.

'Do you know what you're looking like in this light?'

Mamata chose to remain silent.

'Like a bundle of shefali flowers.'

Mamata didn't express her thoughts, and Abu Ibrahim listened to the sound of her breathing, which was gradually getting heavier. Yet, amidst the moonlight and the sound of Mamata's breathing, Abu Ibrahim stayed awake for some more time that night. At eleven the next morning, Khaled Jamil came to his office, and after they exchanged smiles and shook hands, they quickly came to the matter at hand. Khaled Jamil said that the relevant authority had recommended acceptance of his firm Jupiter Enterprises' tender for the import of cement. Abu Ibrahim told him that he had gone through the letter as well as the report comparing the prices proposed by all those who had submitted tenders. He informed him that the price quoted by Jupiter Enterprises was not the lowest, but the second lowest; the tender submitted by the party quoting the lowest price had been rejected on account of being incomplete. And so, he explained, the matter needed to be scrutinized properly. Khaled Jamil nodded gravely as he heard that, and said, 'I won't ask you to do anything untoward. But the rejection of the tender was through proper means.'

His face impassive, Abu Ibrahim said, 'Let's see.' Khaled Jamil then smiled and said, 'Just see what you can do, I need your sympathy.' He got up after that. He shook hands with Abu Ibrahim and left, and then that evening he arrived once again at Abu Ibrahim's residence.

'Have you come to canvas your cause?'

Without any sign of embarrassment, Khaled Jamil retained the smile on his face and said, 'It's not that. How are you?'

'I'm okay.'

'Do you enjoy sitting at home all day?'

'What choice do I have?'

'My wife and I are organizing an outing very soon; we'll be very happy if you, Bhabi and the kids give us company.'

'We'll see.'

Khaled Jamil then looked fixedly at Abu Ibrahim's face and asked, 'Have you examined the proposal?'

'I saw it.'

Khaled Jamil smiled a bit.

'Will we get the business? What do you think?'

'Is it appropriate to talk about it?'

'Please don't take offence.'

Abu Ibrahim was silent, and Kajoli arrived with tea and biscuits. As he sipped the tea, Khaled Jamil insisted, 'In truth, ours is the lowest offer.'

'I don't think so,' Abu Ibrahim replied. Hearing that, Khaled Jamil gazed at him silently for a long while, and then he asked, 'Can we arrive at a deal?'

Abu Ibrahim now had to look directly at Khaled Jamil, into his eyes, and he observed that there were no creases on his face; it was bright and tranquil as always. Khaled Jamil then said, 'I already told you, bhai, that we're in business. We profit from commission, and we don't mind sharing it with friends.'

Abu Ibrahim was still silent, and so Khaled Jamil continued, 'There's no question of any damage or loss to the country or nation associated with this; if you participate, then you also get a benefit, if you don't, then the share of your benefit goes to somebody else. That's what the whole thing is all about, nothing else.'

While Abu Ibrahim felt at a loss for words, Khaled Jamil carried on, 'As far as this tender is concerned, it's our offer that's valid and the lowest. If you recommend acceptance, you wouldn't be doing anything untoward; no one can allege that.'

Abu Ibrahim then responded, 'The offer that's the lowest has been held to be invalid only because of a discrepancy in the packing specifications.'

'But dear sir, if an offer does not adhere to the necessary specifications it's deemed to be invalid. Besides, packing is a very important aspect; the entire consignment of cement could be destroyed on account of poor packing.'

'But one can still ask for the packing specifications to be corrected.'

'That's true. But dear sir, in that case it would be unfair to us. There are rules for everything. The very first stipulation of the tender notice is that the offer must be in accordance with the necessary specifications. If I merely quote the lowest price but make up my own specifications, that can't be acceptable, that would be a joke. Once the tender quotation has been opened, any further negotiations are against both regulations and ethics.'

Abu Ibrahim remained quiet. Lowering his voice, Khaled Jamil once again asked, 'Can we come to a deal?'

'What's that?'

Khaled Jamil pondered for a few moments, and after that he said, 'I hope you won't take it otherwise?'

As Abu Ibrahim waited silently, Khaled Jamil said, 'We can share our profit.' Abu Ibrahim then smiled cheerlessly, and without taking his eyes off him, Khaled Jamil continued, 'You don't have to do anything untoward, only what's fair; and about the profit sharing – actually that money belongs to you; as we are the indenter, a part of our commission is set aside for sharing in this way. It should go to you; you can take it if you like, and if you don't, it stays in our pocket.'

'Is that so?'

Khaled Jamil laughed and said, 'Why not? It's your money.'

Abu Ibrahim realized that he couldn't match this man's complex mesh of words. Weakness and decline gradually devoured him until that day, which suddenly arrived, the day when he once again identified his own beliefs. But until then Khaled Jamil kept advancing, and that day, after hearing that a part of the indenter's commission was due to him, Abu Ibrahim told him, 'I haven't really looked at everything properly as yet.'

'You do that, after all, you have to do that. But as I said, our offer's the lowest. You can definitely recommend the acceptance of the lowest and valid offer.'

'Is that so?' Abu Ibrahim asked with a smile, and Khaled Jamil smiled back in response and said, 'If you don't mind, I shall humbly offer you something.'

'What's that?'

'I'll give you thirty.'

Abu Ibrahim felt a kind of spasm in his shoulder and in the muscle beside his jaw; he furrowed his brow and looked, and seeing that, Khaled Jamil said, 'Don't be offended, please; it's only a gift, I shall give you thirty thousand bucks.'

Abu Ibrahim was silent, he gazed dispiritedly. Khaled Jamil then lit a cigarette and said in his usual voice, 'Okay then, so we are friends, and everything's agreed.'

Abu Ibrahim then said somewhat brusquely, 'I'm not so sure, I have to examine everything thoroughly.'

After Khaled Jamil left that night, Abu Ibrahim had his dinner and watched television silently for a while, and then went to bed. He lay awake all night, and finally, close to dawn, he fell asleep. At the office the next day, he was busy with various things; Khaled Jamil didn't come to meet him again. He felt relieved at that. But even though Khaled Jamil didn't go to Abu Ibrahim's office, he visited him again at his residence in the evening, and he asked, 'Are you annoyed with me?'

'Why?'

'No, just asking.'

Abu Ibrahim then felt mired in a great crisis, and he remained silent, and we can therefore conclude in all propriety that he had taken a decision, and that was why he was silent. We don't really know the reasons behind Abu Ibrahim arriving at the decision; perhaps we'll never know, perhaps in the face of Khaled Jamil's argument it had occurred to him that nothing mattered at all, or perhaps he had something else in mind. But after considering everything, we have no option but to believe that Abu Ibrahim had knowingly made the decision and was waiting for the expected event to occur; although he was also ill at ease inwardly, owing to his inexperience. Looking at his cheerless face that evening, Khaled Jamil lit a cigarette, and he offered Abu Ibrahim one although he knew that he would refuse; he then stretched out his legs in front of him as he blew out a lungful of smoke.

'Have you processed the case?'

'No, I was busy with other work all day.'

'What do you think?'

Abu Ibrahim looked at Khaled Jamil gravely, and Khaled Jamil then took out a fat envelope from his trouser pocket and put it on top of the table. We can't tell whether there was dejection or delight in Abu Ibrahim's gaze when he looked at the envelope on the table. However, we keep observing the entirety of his downfall; looking him in the face, Khaled Jamil blurted out, 'Please ... please, you deserve it, it's the whole thirty thousand.' Nevertheless, Abu Ibrahim did not don a pleased look even after that; he said rather dully, 'I've already said that I have to examine the matter thoroughly.' It then seemed that, just like Newton discovered the law of gravity when he observed a falling object, similarly, looking at the falling Abu Ibrahim, Khaled Jamil intuited a law of human behaviour. He said, 'You don't have to do anything untoward.' After Khaled Jamil left Abu Ibrahim's residence that evening, Abu Ibrahim sat impassively for a while at first, and then he picked up the bundle of money, went to the bedroom, put the envelope inside the drawer of the steel cupboard and locked it, and after that, he went and stood in the balcony like he did every day, and as he gazed at the cluster of trees on Minto Road, he mentally examined the documents in his office, and it occurred to him that the price proposed by Khaled Jamil's firm was not the lowest, it was the second lowest, and compared to the rejected lowest tender, the price was two dollars more per ton. A flying insect then landed on his face, and as he brushed it away with his hand, he calculated that, for the required quantity of ten thousand tons, the difference amounted to twenty thousand dollars, and he thought that was a lot of money. Bindu and Shubho then returned and sat down to study, and Abu Ibrahim sat down near them and scanned the newspaper once again. And as he cast his eyes over the cinema advertisements in the entertainment section, it struck him that if the party offering the lowest tender price was given an opportunity, all that money could be saved. He then remembered the envelope left behind by Khaled Jamil, and he went over the whole thing once again, in a different way. As Mamata helped Shubho do his sums, she asked Abu Ibrahim whether he planned to go to her father's house. He didn't answer her clearly. He kept wondering whether he needed to go to his father-in-law at all for the money to buy the plot in Rupnagar when he had thirty thousand taka in cash. But he thought that Khaled Jamil ought not to get this business contract. He then went over the whole thing yet again. In this way, he fell into a kind of obsession, and

when Bindu and Shubho finished their studies, they all
had dinner, and after watching television for a little while,
when everyone had gone to bed, he was still immersed in
thinking about the cement purchase proposal. The next day,
as soon as he reached the office, he sat down with the file
and once again examined everything minutely, and then,
like a rapturous revelation, he found a solution. He called
his steno-typist at once and dictated a note, and after that,
at around ten in the morning, Khaled Jamil phoned him.

'How are you, bhai?'

'I'm okay, how are you?'

'Yes, I'm fine.' Abu Ibrahim then suddenly heard
Khaled Jamil's voice turn resonant, 'I am very happy.'

'Why?'

'No, it's nothing like that. By the way, have you looked
at the file?'

'Yes, the note's being typed.'

'Is everything all right?'

'Yes.'

'So Jupiter Enterprises is getting the business?'

'Yes, but the price has to be adjusted to match the
lowest price.'

'There you go, finishing me off…'

'There's no option.'

'Please think about it. This isn't possible; my principal
will not agree. We'll incur a heavy loss.'

'I can't see any way out.'

'Still, think about it once again. You can straightaway propose that the offer made by Jupiter Enterprises be accepted.'

'No, I can't. The contract can be awarded to the lowest bidder as well; the discrepancy in the packing specifications is absolutely insignificant. That matter can still be negotiated, and if that's done, it comes to twenty thousand dollars less. And so, let your Jupiter Enterprises get the contract, but it would be appropriate if the price is brought down by two dollars. I'm sure you can understand my situation.'

Khaled Jamil pleaded, 'Still, look at it once again,' and disconnected, and Abu Ibrahim didn't think about the matter any more. When the note for the cement purchase file was typed, he put it into the file and went to attend a meeting, and after the meeting was over he returned home. As he sat down for lunch that day, he informed Mamata about the existence of the thirty thousand taka, and when she asked about its source, he said, 'I took a house building advance.' He added that he had to obtain another ten thousand taka and that he might have to go to her father's house very soon on that account. He had no further conversation with Mamata regarding the money for buying the plot of land and going to his in-laws' house. That afternoon, after telling Mamata about his upcoming trip, he took a short nap. The next day, Khaled Jamil arrived at his office and observed that the file was still lying

on Abu Ibrahim's table. Khaled Jamil flashed a smile of
great confidence and shook the grim-faced Abu Ibrahim's
hand for an exceedingly long time.

'How are you?'

Even after all that had transpired, Abu Ibrahim
couldn't regain his confidence, he squinted his eyes and
curved his lips into a smile; he couldn't let himself go, and
he replied starchily, 'I'm fine. Are you well?'

'Yes, have you put up the file?'

'No, the file's here, I will be putting it up.'

'Is it whatever you said?'

'Yes.' And then, as if in justification, he drily added,
'You can understand, I'm merely an employee.'

Khaled Jamil smiled a bit by mistake when he heard
that, and he continued making mistakes in this way, or
to put it differently, it was as if in this way he moved
from one identity to another, and unfortunately Abu
Ibrahim identified him from the margin of his abandoned
consciousness. He did not like the smile on Khaled Jamil's
face, and he thought he ought not to have sought to justify
himself. But Khaled Jamil could not comprehend Abu
Ibrahim. He extended his right hand and placed it on the
table, and then he looked at Abu Ibrahim's face and asked,
'Why do you fear your job so much?'

Confronted with this question, Abu Ibrahim curved
his lips helplessly into a smile.

'Your job doesn't provide you anything. And yet you're always worried about it.'

When Abu Ibrahim still remained silent after that, Khaled Jamil said with greater enthusiasm, 'One has to take risks in life without being afraid.'

'Is that so?'

'No one loses their job; if that were the case, no one in this country would remain employed.'

'Yet jobs are lost too,' Abu Ibrahim argued.

'All right then. But even if it is so, what's the harm in that? I've never had a job, have I come to any harm because of that?'

'Not everyone can do business.'

'Yes, that's true.' Khaled Jamil then lit a cigarette, took a deep puff, and said, 'Have you ever thought of getting into business?'

'Everyone who is employed thinks of getting into business.'

'That's right. What's your view about business?'

'It's difficult.'

In the course of talking, Khaled Jamil had probably unfastened his bolt of caution, because he said, 'It is very challenging, I enjoy that. It's a sort of game. I can pursue anybody. I can get a job done under any circumstances.'

'Really!'

'It's really true. Everyone is manageable, and everybody can be purchased.'

Thus did Khaled Jamil utter this final sentence, without much caution and care, and as a result, even as Abu Ibrahim sat in his office which lacked natural light and ventilation, he simultaneously visualized Khaled Jamil and himself standing in an altered frame, and in reversed roles. Khaled Jamil took a few moments to think over the matter, and then said almost immediately, 'Please don't mind. You are my friend.' They sat for a long while without saying anything. After that, Khaled Jamil said, 'Will you be releasing the file today?'

'Yes.'

Khaled Jamil didn't lose his confidence; he smiled, shook hands and left. Abu Ibrahim remained sitting there, and as he figured out the whole situation, he became increasingly perturbed. He put the file relating to the cement purchase inside the cupboard, locked it and left for Siddiq Hossain's office. After Abu Ibrahim's death, for no reason at all, Siddiq Hossain remembered this day; he recalled that his ever-dejected face looked as still and impassive as the surface of a pond on a summer's day. Perhaps that was on account of some more depression, disappointment or some kind of yearning, because Siddiq Hossain recalled that, on that day, Abu Ibrahim had declared in a somewhat delirious yet calm and quiet voice, 'I am a bastard!' After leaving Siddiq Hossain's office that day, he returned to his residence before noon, and saying he had a headache, he took two tablets of Disprin and lay down. This headache persisted all day and all night. Before going to his office the next day, he took two more Disprins dissolved in water. When he reached the office, he sat down with the file relating to the cement purchase and completed his task quickly. He tore up the note in the file that he had written earlier, called the stenographer and dictated, and when the new note was typed, he signed it and released the file. Then, around nine, he left and went over to Siddiq Hossain's office, and had tea and chatted. Returning to his own office room at twelve, he found Khaled Jamil sitting there, and he thought to himself that he knew this man would be waiting for him. Khaled Jamil's face broke into a smile upon seeing him, and he asked, 'Where had you gone?'

Abu Ibrahim said, 'Just nearby...'

'Have you released the file?'

'Yes.'

Khaled Jamil beamed from ear to ear and said, 'All right.' After that, he picked up his shiny, black briefcase and got ready to leave. Abu Ibrahim then looked indifferently at his face, and Khaled Jamil met his gaze by once again spreading out the plumage of his ghoulish smile. Lowering his eyes, Abu Ibrahim said in muted tones, 'Actually, I went through the whole proposal and all the papers once again.'

Khaled Jamil did not change his demeanour when he heard Abu Ibrahim; he continued to stare at him in the same way. Abu Ibrahim then averted his eyes once again and said, 'The lowest bidder ought to be given an opportunity to correct the packing specifications, and if he agrees to do that, he should be awarded the contract. It's only if he doesn't agree that negotiations can be carried out with the second lowest bidder for price adjustment.'

Even as he said that, Abu Ibrahim didn't discern any trace of an abnormal reaction from Khaled Jamil, who only said, 'I can't understand what you're saying.'

'That's what's fair,' Abu Ibrahim said. Khaled Jamil's face then gradually took on a confused look, and he remarked, 'Is that so?'

'That's what I think.'

'So what did you write in the file?'

'What I just said.'

'Are you sure?'

'Yes.'

It then occurred to Abu Ibrahim that what he was observing on Khaled Jamil's face was merely disappointment. Khaled Jamil asked him in an astonishingly weary voice, 'Why did you do this?'

'That's what was fair.'

Khaled Jamil was upset and silent for a while, and then he asked, 'Are you giving the money back?'

'What money?'

Khaled Jamil thought that Abu Ibrahim hadn't understood him, so he furrowed his brow and stared at him. When we learn about this matter, Abu Ibrahim's behaviour might seem incomprehensible to us as well. But we can assume that perhaps he had made a calculation in this regard too. After asking 'What money?' he fixed his gaze on Khaled Jamil's face and observed that the two corners of his lips were pressed tight. But even before he could fully enjoy the composition of this scene of the drama, he was filled with astonishment and anxiety to see Khaled Jamil shake himself out of his state of bewilderment, say, 'All right, I'll see you again,' and leave. Abu Ibrahim had a lot to ponder over then, and the first thing he thought about was that Khaled Jamil wouldn't go to the police, and he wouldn't complain to the higher authorities either. But what he could not figure out was what Khaled Jamil would actually do now. That was the situation when Khaled Jamil phoned him the next day.

'This is Khaled speaking.'

'Yes.'

'Has the file come back?'

'No.'

'Now tell me about the money you have taken.'

'What money?'

'Don't you know?'

'Tell me.'

'Listen gentleman, you are playing with fire.'

'I'm busy now, I have to go.'

Khaled Jamil was silent, and Abu Ibrahim hung up. The next day, Abu Ibrahim took leave for two days and

went to his in-laws' house, and told his father-in-law to
arrange for forty thousand taka. Going to his office the
following Monday, he found that the file pertaining to the
cement purchase had come back, and he observed that what
he had suggested had been approved. Abu Ibrahim wrote
a letter informing the Trading Corporation of Bangladesh
about this decision, and a little while later he received a
phone call from Khaled Jamil. 'You've double-crossed me.'

'Don't talk rubbish.'

'You have to pay the price for that.'

'Don't try to frighten me.'

'Okay, I want my money back.'

'What money are you talking about?'

'You don't know me, Ibrahim sahib, please don't pull
my leg.'

'Sorry, I have to go.'

Abu Ibrahim disconnected the telephone, and began
working on a file, and after some time Khaled Jamil arrived
and entered his room. Abu Ibrahim's heart began to beat
faster when he saw him, but he managed to maintain his
composure and observed that Khaled Jamil's face was still
and looked ominous, like a dark cloud. Khaled Jamil asked
Abu Ibrahim in English why he was playing this game, and
his frustration and agitation increased when Abu Ibrahim
replied that he couldn't understand what he was saying.
Khaled Jamil then composed himself and said, 'All right.

I admit that I didn't understand either. Now I want my money back.'

'What money are you talking about?'

Bolts of lightning flashed in Khaled Jamil's clouded face; he pursed his lips, pushed the chair back with a jerk, and got up and left. The next day, quite early in the morning, before the office filled up with people, Khaled Jamil arrived and entered Abu Ibrahim's room, and without saying a word he sat down on the chair in front of his table. Abu Ibrahim got somewhat scared, but there was nothing he could do other than wait quietly.

'I want to know your real intention.'

'About what?'

Abu Ibrahim was terrified that Khaled Jamil would finally explode into a million pieces if he told him. But Khaled Jamil kept his cool even then, his eyelids fluttered, and when he tried to stop the fluttering, the corners of his eyes creased, and he muttered, 'About the money you took from me.'

'I did not take any money from you, please tell me properly.'

Khaled Jamil clenched his fist which lay on the table, then unclenched it and said, 'Okay, okay, about the money I gave you.'

But Abu Ibrahim did not appear to be satisfied even after Khaled Jamil said that; it seemed he wanted to drag

Khaled Jamil towards some finale, and so he asked, 'What money? Why would you give me any money?'

Khaled Jamil's eyes remained screwed; he said, 'You don't want to give my money back?'

'What are you saying? What money of yours?'

Khaled Jamil bit his lip once again and said in exasperation, 'I gave it as a bribe! You took a bribe from me, but you didn't do the job.'

Abu Ibrahim gazed at Khaled Jamil's face, and when in addition to rage, a look of frustration began to appear on it, he said, 'So you give bribes!'

Khaled Jamil was silent, after that he said, 'You are just playing a useless game.'

'Why not!'

'Won't you give my money back?'

Abu Ibrahim then lowered his face, nodded and said, 'Yes, I will.'

Perhaps out of bewilderment, or for some other reason, Khaled Jamil was at a loss for words, and he waited, but when Abu Ibrahim didn't say anything more, he asked, 'Shall I come to your residence?'

'No.'

'Then?'

'I'll bring it and give it to you.'

'When?'

'Tomorrow.'

'Shall I come here?'

'No, don't come here. Wait in front of the General Post Office at ten in the morning tomorrow, I'll be there.'

Khaled Jamil could not fathom why Abu Ibrahim had been so immoderate, and perhaps we too won't be able to comprehend Abu Ibrahim. In fact, even before we could give it a try, in less than twenty-four hours, he came face to face with death. It was a Tuesday, and as he was leaving for office in the morning, Abu Ibrahim took out the envelope containing thirty thousand taka and put it inside his folio-bag; he told Mamata that he had to give the money to someone, and before Mamata could say anything, he left home. After that, when the watch on his wrist showed ten o'clock, he went and stood in front of the GPO with the envelope containing the money stuffed inside his pocket. But he did not find Khaled Jamil there. As he waited, after some time, two youths suddenly emerged as if they had burst out of the earth and came and stood in front of him, and said to him in whispers, 'Give us whatever you have.' Abu Ibrahim had only a moment to be startled, and after that, three things happened in a single moment. When one of the youths tugged his arm and inserted his hand inside his bulging trouser-pocket, Abu Ibrahim said, 'Hey,' and just then the second youth raised his right hand; Abu Ibrahim saw only a glint of silver flashing in the sunlight, and even before he could say a word or make any sound, the youth planted the blade of his dagger in the left side of Abu

Ibrahim's chest, into his heart. By the time Abu Ibrahim could understand anything, his life was extinguished. The two youths held his limp body and laid it down on the road, and before the people nearby could figure out what had happened, they ran away in the direction of Baitul Mukarram.

And thus was Abu Ibrahim devoured by a death that was lighter and more insignificant than a goose feather, and thus we have no further interest in him; but we are surprised by that. It seems that only his fat wife Mamata couldn't give him up. She kept weaving a kind of design for survival, centring around his grave. Mamata took Abu Ibrahim's dead body to Sirajganj and buried it there; she got Bindu and Shubho admitted to a local school. Abu Ibrahim's grave in the Hossainpur cemetery in the suburbs of Sirajganj town was carpeted with green grass, and on rainy days, bunches of red flowers bloomed on the shimul trees planted at the four corners of the grave. Mamata came regularly with Bindu and Shubho and attended to the grave. Her aged father was stricken with sorrow owing to Mamata's depression, and grief cast its shadow on their whole family. Proposals for another marriage arrived for the young widow, but she did not consent, and in this way, two years went by after Abu Ibrahim's death. Abdul Hakim was the elder brother of Mamata's friend, Shefali, from the Dhanbandhi locality. His wife passed away, and a few months after that, Shefali prevailed upon Mamata's father to get her married to Abdul Hakim. As all of them tried to convince Mamata, her aged father lay all day on the canvas easy chair in the veranda, gazing at the sky. Mamata thought long over the matter, but couldn't arrive at a decision. After that, she had a heated altercation with her elder brother, and as the world slumbered, she wept fervently all night long. Three days after Mamata had wept all night, she got married to Shefali's elder brother, and the very next day, Shefali's elder brother left with them for his workplace in Khulna. Mamata wiped her tears, and holding Shubho's and Bindu's hands, boarded the train, and she then saw Abdul Hakim trying to wipe the tears streaming down Bindu's face with his hand. When the train left the Sirajganj Bazar station in the wan light of late afternoon, looking at Abdul Hakim and at Bindu who was enclosed in his arms, her eyes brimmed with tears once again. As the train rumbled past a culvert, blew its horn and sped ahead, in the Hossainpur cemetery, a dog carrying the discarded entrails of a cow in its mouth sat down near Abu Ibrahim's grave. A second dog followed behind the first, and after that the two dogs growled and began fighting, their loud barks shattering the silence of the cemetery. Then, in the midst of the fighting, one dog grabbed the pieces of the entrails in its mouth and dragged them away, and the silence of slumber once again descended upon the desolate cemetery; the evening's breeze turned chilly and pleasant. A full moon rose from behind a faraway building, and remained suspended like a gas balloon in the gap between the leaves of a koroi tree, and an owl came flying in the pale moonlight, sat on a branch of a shimul tree and looked this way and that. After that, when the owl suddenly flew away and then pounced down upon the grass, a mole shrieked and scurried through the jungle of weeds, and the owl followed it zigzaggedly, swooping down again and again.

AND THUS DO WE FORGET about the grave in the cemetery; the moon smiled down on it from the cloudless sky, the air resounded with the shrieks of the mole, and the owl flapped its wings and flew around all night long.

Translator's Afterword

I LEARNT THE NAME OF Shahidul Zahir in March 2019 from Iqbal Hasnu, a Bangladeshi, the editor of the bilingual *Bangla Journal* published from Toronto, Canada. We had become (electronically) acquainted through common friends, and thus began a literary friendship. My translation of an anti-story by Subimal Misra was carried in the 2018 issue of his literary journal. After that, Iqbal wrote to me: 'I would like you to read the late Bangladeshi writer, Shahidul Zahir, whose writing demands an eye like yours for translation, and who you may find quite extraordinary!' He then had a collection of Zahir's short stories sent to me from Dhaka, Bangladesh. Not long after that, another literary friend, Ajmal Kamal, from Karachi, Pakistan, a co-editor of the South Asian literary journal, *City*, wrote to me, urging my contribution, via translation, to the journal's issue on contemporary writing from Bangladesh. He then sent me soft copies of short stories by some contemporary Bangladeshi authors, and among them were some by Shahidul Zahir. The name rang a bell, and I realized it was the same author Iqbal had mentioned. And thus I began reading his stories, and was immediately ensnared by the magic of his prose; I couldn't stop myself from sitting down to translate almost at once. I translated the short story, 'The Fig-Eating Folk', for *City: 7*. And then 'The Woodcutter and the Ravens', which was published in *Bangla Journal*. But I realized I needed to get the consent of the late author's estate, and once again, thanks to Iqbal, the connection was established.

By then I had read two collections of stories Zahir had published, i.e., *Dumurkheko Manush* (1999) and *Dolu Nodir Haowa* (2004), as well as his novella, *Jibon O Rajnoitik Bastobota* (1987), and the novel, *Mukher Dike Dekhi* (2006). Shahidul Zahir is the first Bengali author that I read in Bangla for the sheer pleasure of reading, and I read him with the same voraciousness with which I had entered the life and world of reading over fifty years ago, and the same 'double take' I experienced on reading *The Tin Drum*, by Günter Grass, at age twenty: 'So this is what they call literature!' For about two weeks, I lived in his writing. The names of writers as diverse as Isaac Bashevis Singer, R.K. Narayan and José Saramago, among others, came to mind. But notwithstanding all those resonances, my sense was that the roots of Shahidul Zahir's literary work were entirely indigenous, planted deep in the soil of Bangladesh; they are one sample of the literary genius arisen from the soil of this nation born in genocide. I also read some essays about Shahidul Zahir's work, and thus became aware that his name is actually held in high regard in Bangladesh and West Bengal. But although he has a large following in these reading spaces, it would not be incorrect to say that his name is still not so well known. And of course, his writing had not been translated.

I requested the late author's estate to grant me consent to translate Zahir's work. When I received their go-ahead and encouragement, I was over the moon, deeply humbled, and sworn into whatever it might take to do justice to the task.

I HAD BEEN A KIND of devotee of the American writer, J.D. Salinger. In my mind, there is a certain similarity between him and Shahidul Zahir. Both were writers of works that had an amazing, hypnotic effect on readers, and both of them had a small body of published work. In the case of Salinger, that was by choice, as he moved to a reclusive life from the pinnacle of success and stopped publishing; in Zahir's case, his mostly unknown, unread, small oeuvre was all that remained when he died prematurely, and his renown is almost entirely posthumous.

Shahidul Zahir was truly a brilliant shooting star in the literary firmament of Bangladesh and the world. A natural storyteller, writing prose about and in the contemporary while evoking the timeless oral tradition.

I was an eleven-year-old boy in Calcutta in 1971, at the time of the genocide in East Pakistan, and the Liberation War for Bangladesh made a deep mark on me, as it did on an entire generation worldwide. Who can forget Swadhin Bangla Betar (Free Bangladesh Radio)? The Concert for Bangladesh (organized by Ravi Shankar and George Harrison)? 'The Story of Bangladesh' sung by Joan Baez? The poem 'September on Jessore Road' by Allen Ginsberg, and the song 'Jessore Road' based on it sung by Moushumi Bhowmick? My aunt, Indu Nagpaul, a thirty-year-old physician in the UK, joined a team of volunteer doctors and nurses organized by War on Want, and came to Calcutta where she worked for a few months in the refugee camp in Salt Lake – an experience that I believe was so traumatic that she never spoke about it to anyone. I have a photograph of her having successfully delivered a baby in the refugee camp. *Jibon O Rajnoitik Bastobota* is about 1971.

As a translator of voices from the margins of Bengali literature, I thought that by translating *Jibon O Rajnoitik Bastobota*, I could pay homage to the sacred memory of the birth of Bangladesh, to the late author, and the founding ideals of the nation – at the root of which was a love of the Bengali language, now imperilled in my own India with the growing onslaught of Hindi imperialism under the Hindu majoritarian central government. But more significantly, the world of literature is largely unaware of the unique literary genius of this country – principally on account of the acute paucity of good translations. This is my personal effort, in an activist vein as it were, towards filling that void, and I do that with an exceptional writer, a modern and deeply *political* writer – of and from the post-colonial Global South; someone the wider world of literature would want to draw close. Zahir symbolizes and represents the independent literary voice, vision and verve of post-1971 Bangladesh.

I had also come to realize that as a literary translator of powerful, creative voices in Bangla, it was vital for me to start looking at Bangladesh (rather than the Indian state of West Bengal where I live). And that it is the people of Bangladesh who are today the Bengali nation and the custodians of the Bengali language. And so, the Zahir stimulus resulted in my initiating an ongoing personal engagement with Bangladesh and its people, and the literary world there. That has been a rich and ever-expanding experience.

IN EARLY 2020, I ASKED Shahroza Nahrin, with whom I became acquainted through social media, whether she would join me as a co-translator. And thus I arrived in Dhaka in February 2020, and spent about a week working on the first round of translation with Shahroza; she read out, and I wrote out the translation, sentence by sentence. And in her absence, my young friend, Ijtehad Sayeed, a marine biologist, assisted me. A first draft was completed.

I am grateful to Prof. Shamsad Mortuza of the University of Liberal Arts, Bangladesh, for the kind and generous hospitality offered me, which enabled the first draft of *Life and Political Reality* to be completed.

I remember, one sentence took me a long time to figure out, in terms of what exactly it meant, and how it might be expressed in English. I grappled with it for quite a while, and then I stopped and went and lay down. Shortly after that, in a 'eureka' moment, I leapt out of bed, shouted out to Ijtehad – 'I've got it!' – and wrote it down. 'In that afternoon laden with melancholy, seeing the skulls arrayed over banana leaves, the people of the moholla had imagined an exquisitely woven jamdani sari, and now, it was in that jamdani sari that they saw their mothers and lovers, their daughters and daughters' daughters attired whenever they gathered during the various festivals of life.'

In *Jibon O Rajnoitik Bastobota*, there is only a little bit of direct speech, most of the narrative is in indirect speech. And while the latter is mostly written in 'standard Bangla', the former is in dialect. The different dialects or speeches of East Bengal, that is Bangladesh, have held a special allure for me from my childhood. And so, I decided to Romanize and reproduce the direct speech wherever it occurs. So that the 'people's voice' appears in the translation. For the reader of the Bangla original, the use of dialect has a polychromatic effect, while a translation into English can only be monochromatic. Transcribing the speech into Roman was the only means I could think of towards addressing the challenge of untranslatability of dialect.

Before I left Dhaka, Shahroza and her friend, Nabeel, took me on a tour of Puran Dhaka, or the Old City, pointing to all the places and spots mentioned in *Life and Political Reality*, and memorialized through a lot of Shahidul Zahir's writing. I am truly fortunate – as someone born in a Tamil family in India – to have been able to gain access to so much, in such little time. The investment I made, of idealistic aspiration, yielded returns beyond counting. But that is because of language, as well the special soil of Bangladesh, and her people.

I visited Chittagong after that, and there I met Prof. Masud Mahmood, formerly of the Department of English at Chittagong University. Actually, Prof. Masud Mahmood was the first person to translate *Jibon O Rajnoitik Bastobota* into English. My friend Alam Khorshed, essayist, translator and arts organizer, had told me that, and Prof. Masud's former student, Khan Touseef Osman, helped me to get in touch with him. Sadly, his translation has remained unpublished. He showed me his manuscript, and I would like to acknowledge here that I thought to add the word *'phot'* – which appears in the very first sentence of *Life and Political Reality* (and also one more time, later) – only after glancing through the first page of Prof. Masud's manuscript. I am indebted to him.

MY FLATMATE AT THE ULAB guest house in Dhaka was Dr Chris Moffat, a historian, from Queen Mary University of London, and author of the book, *India's Revolutionary Inheritance: Politics and the Promise of Bhagat Singh* (2019). He was in Bangladesh in connection with his research work on the architecture of postcolonial development in Karachi and Dhaka. We chatted about *Life and Political Reality* in the evenings, and once the draft was done, I sent it to him. He wrote back:

> I sat down with it today and was absolutely gripped, till the end. I really like the tangled temporality of it – the opening *snap*, the shift back in time, then forward, then back again, then a slight return, etc., etc., all woven together in this truly powerful way.
>
> I think you mentioned to me at one point in Dhaka, the way Zahir thought about history – this line stood out to my own interests, especially: 'But the people of Lakshmi Bazar who kept on forgetting the past saw that their past broke unremittingly through the soil and sprang up, like shoots of grass.'
>
> But I was most captivated by the novella's portrait of the collaborator, the traitor, Moulana Bodu. My favourite moment has to be the Pakistani captain's luxurious piss – 'The sound of the pissing occupied his entire auditory faculty, and the captain executed

the act with such luxury that it seemed like he would continue to do the deed eternally, and that the dull sound of the captain pissing, which occupied Moulana Bodu's entire consciousness, would waft like a faint melody all his life.' Indeed, this moment provides such perfect comic insight into this dark history of collaboration – people thought Moulana Bodu had thrown out the grey clothes, as it appeared the captain had wiped his piss-flecked hand on them, but in fact, he had saved them as a memento!

I'm glad to have seen Old Dhaka and read the story through those streets and places, though Zahir's text does evoke this world in unexpected ways – particularly the scene of the razakars' offensive against plant life...

There is a quiet rage and fury throughout the text, which I see was written in the late-1980s, with 1971 still relatively recent. It will be interesting to know how it is received now – especially those points about the inability to *really* forget, the corruption of what came after independence, the perils of amnesty ... which must resonate, even if in different ways.

It is a wonderful story, and it is a pleasure, too, to have lived in proximity to the act of translation, and I certainly recognized bits and pieces from our conversations.

Chris's response assured me that my translation was reasonably competent. But much more work remained to be done. Given the nature and stature of the original text, it demanded a great deal of dedication and conscientiousness on the part of a translator.

I RETURNED TO KOLKATA IN early March – and then came COVID-19 and the lockdown, which stalled everything. In September 2020, Shahroza and I resumed our work, now through online communication. And thus, over a two-month period, we went over the novella several times, comparing it with the translation, all the while poring over the manuscript, fishing for things to examine, correct, polish, etc., until the final manuscript was completed in November.

Every reading brought new revelations, which Shahroza and I discussed, towards resolving doubts and queries. Zahir is a writer who demands exacting zeal and labour from a translator, because every word and sentence, and the whole structure of the work, is exquisitely sculpted into one seamless whole. Our love of Zahir's prose drove us to carry out that patient, unstinting and devoted labour, without which the translation would be flawed.

Commenting on the translation of *Life and Political Reality*, Shruti Debi, my literary agent, said it was all about cadence, and that I had got it right. I could just as well have got it wrong, for all I knew. All I was doing was hearing the Bangla and rendering that into English as accurately as possible, while adhering to acceptable English usage and stretching the limits of syntax as far as possible.

LIFE AND POLITICAL REALITY IS a 'slim' novella, and so my editor at HarperCollins, Rahul Soni, asked for 'more' so that it could make up a book, and thus I thought to add the second novella in this volume, *Abu Ibrahimer Mrityu* (first published in 1991, in the little magazine, *Nipun*). I had not originally intended to translate it, and so I hadn't read it. I only read it in March 2021 and then began translating it. But before that, I had read the essay, 'Reading Shahidul Zahir, Reading *Jibon O Rajnoitik Bastobota*' by the literature scholar, Dr Sarker Hasan Al Zayed (which accompanies the Bangladesh edition of *Life and Political Reality*), in which he had mentioned *Abu Ibrahimer Mrityu*:

> In 1991, Zahir followed up his quasi-magic realist first novella with another novella, titled *Abu Ibrahimer Mrityu* (Abu Ibrahim's Death) – a social realist narrative about the tragic death of a middle-class government employee. First published in a magazine, this subtle exploration of the private world of an 'inconsequential man' showcases its writer's masterful

command over evocative language. Subdued and almost understated, the barebones narrative of Zahir's second major novella harmoniously complements its elegiac content. Like García Márquez's *Chronicle of a Death Foretold*, *Abu Ibrahimer Mrityu* too announces the death of its protagonist in the opening lines of the novel, foreshadowing what is to come. The inconsequential death that is announced at the beginning gradually metamorphoses into an acutely consequential one – for the family whose emotional fabric is torn asunder by the protagonist's catastrophic death, and for the corrupt society which loses a heroic naysayer – when one weighs in the symbolic import of losing Abu Ibrahim in the context of the corrupt socioeconomic culture of post-Liberation War Bangladesh. Abu Ibrahim symbolizes the resistance against the ascending neoliberal order which mandates the placing of personal gain before all ideals and values. The titular irony, which initially appears like a celebration of the trivial, thus catapults into an elegiac lamentation when one reads Abu Ibrahim's death from the vantage points of his society's and family's loss.

So I was keen to take it up. After I read *Abu Ibrahimer Mrityu*, I was certain it would be a good complement to

Life and Political Reality. Like I did with the latter, I sent my draft of *Abu Ibrahim's Death* to Shahroza for scrutiny, and we went over it several times through online meetings, until it was completed in June.

IN LATE 1967, RETURNING FROM Europe, where my father had gone for a few months' training, my mother had brought back a (45 rpm) record of The Beatles' song 'Hello, Goodbye', which was all the rage there at that time. On its B-side was the song, 'I Am the Walrus'. A few years later, a cousin gifted me the Simon & Garfunkel record, 'Bridge Over Troubled Water'. On its B-side was the song, 'Keep the Customer Satisfied'. It's only the A-side song that's listened to and remembered!

In translation, *Abu Ibrahim's Death* might be fated to be like the B-side of *Life and Political Reality*. But that would not do it justice. It is a moving story, and one that broadens the canvas of one's perspective on Shahidul Zahir and his writing. I was reminded of Kenzaburō Ōe's 'quiet' sequel to his full-blown novel, *Rouse Up O Young Men of the New Age!*, titled *A Quiet Life*, an accomplished work in its own right within Kenzaburō Ōe's oeuvre. Reading the two, one after the other, was also an experience in itself.

I realized that there is something beyond a powerful work, which can overwhelm a reader. A 'quiet' work also reveals the writer's literary imagination and craft, and the two together tell us something about the writer's range of capability. Rahul Soni, my editor at HarperCollins, responded after reading *Abu Ibrahim's Death*: 'What a pleasure it was to read and work on this. And you're right, a much quieter (albeit not gentler) work, this one, yet still very Shahidul Zahir and all so very recognizable and true.' So I would like to think that there need not be an 'A-side' or a 'B-side' in literature, and that the novellas brought together in this volume will enable a very rich reading experience.

SHAHROZA TOLD ME THAT SHE thought of translating *Jibon O Rajnoitik Bastobota* when she watched the stage rendition of the novella, directed by Syed Jamil Ahmed, in Dhaka in 2019. I learnt about that production in 2019 from my friend, Alam Khorshed, and then I was able to get in touch with him in 2020, thanks to the political activist and publisher, Zonayed Saki, and also finally meet him in Dhaka in 2021. Jamil Ahmed contributed an essay titled, '*Jibon O Rajnoitik Bastobota*: Translation from a Novella to a Theatre Production', which accompanies the Bangladesh edition of *Life and Political Reality*. He wrote:

> ... [O]nce I began, I could not bring myself to pause, and had to read it through to the end. The opening

image – of the sandal-strap snapping and crows flying in the sky – did it for me. It was so powerful and moving that I was actually glued to it, and the novella sped through my consciousness at a breathtaking, meteoric speed, etching an excruciating and raw sense of unrelenting, wrenching pain somewhere deep inside my being. Soon, there was a huge pain welling up as I read about Momena's death, and her younger brother retrieving her body from a silver stretch of the riverbank at Rayer Bazar. I cannot recall having ever been touched and pained so profoundly, in reading a work of fiction. Momena was indelibly imprinted in my mind. Ever since then, *Jibon O Rajnoitik Bastobota* haunted me unremittingly.

So I am indeed happy that Shahroza was able to work on this book with me. We have grown together in many ways through this experience. Working with her taught me that 'two is better than one', and her dedication, ownership of the project, and painstaking partnership has been truly wonderful to behold. She contributed several gems to the translation, among them the word 'sable' for the Bangla 'krishnoborno'. I have decided that, henceforth, I will work with young translators, and I hope this will serve as a starting point for them to practise and propagate the noble vocation of translation. Bengali literature, and Bangladesh in particular, needs an army of translators – a new Mukti Bahini of literature as it were – who will carry the fair name of Bangladesh to the world stage as valiantly as their forebears liberated the nation.

V. Ramaswamy
Kolkata, September 2021

SHAHIDUL ZAHIR (1953–2008) completed his post-graduation at the University of Dhaka and the American University, Washington D.C., and joined the civil services in Bangladesh. He is best known for his novella, *Jibon O Rajnoitik Bastobota*. Shahidul Zahir's oeuvre includes the short story collections *Parapar, Dumurkheko Manush O Onyanno Golpo*, and *Dolu Nodir Haowa O Onyanno Golpo*, the novels *Shey Raate Purnima Chhilo* and *Mukher Dike Dekhi*, and the novella *Abu Ibrahimer Mrityu*.

V. RAMASWAMY has translated Subimal Misra's *The Golden Gandhi Statue from America: Early Stories*, *Wild Animals Prohibited: Stories, Anti-Stories*, and *This Could Have Become Ramayan Chamar's Tale: Two Anti-Novels*. His translation of *The Runaway Boy* by Manoranjan Byapari was published in 2020.

SHAHROZA NAHRIN is currently pursuing a graduate degree at McGill University, Canada. Her translations include works by Shahidul Zahir and Anwara Syed Haq.